The Ghost of Craven Cove

Nancy and George quickly started to scale the cliff. But when they looked up, they could see only jagged mounds of rock poking out of the gathering mist.

"I hope Laura's not *there*," said Nancy. "It would be hard to climb up or down. I—"

Suddenly a horrible scream ripped through the air. "Help!"

"Laura!" Nancy shouted. "Is that you?"

Through the swirling mist Laura's terrified voice echoed back. "Nancy, I'm falling! Help me!"

Nancy and George scrambled up the rocks and made their way along the ledge to the far end. There they found Laura, hanging on the edge of the cliff by her fingertips.

She was desperately trying to hold on. Twenty feet below, the sea crashed against the rocky shore. . . .

Nancy Drew
Mystery Stories

Available from MINSTREL Books

NANCY DREW MYSTERY STORIES®

92

NANCY DREW®

THE GHOST OF CRAVEN COVE

CAROLYN KEENE

A MINSTREL® BOOK

PUBLISHED BY POCKET BOOKS

New York   London   Toronto   Sydney   Tokyo   Singapore

A MINSTREL PAPERBACK *ORIGINAL*

A Minstrel Book published by
POCKET BOOKS, a division of Simon & Schuster
1230 Avenue of the Americas, New York, NY 10020

ISBN: 0-671-66317-8

First Minstrel Books printing December 1989

10 9 8 7 6 5 4 3

Contents

1

A Call for Help

"I can't believe it," said Nancy Drew, sticking her head out the car window. She took a deep breath as the salty air whipped through her reddish blond hair and sent a tingle of excitement through her body. "Seven whole days in Maine!"

"I know what you mean," Bess Marvin agreed from the back seat. "Nothing but sunshine, the seashore, fresh air—"

"And all the lobsters you can eat," eighteen-year-old George Fayne teased as she steered their rented car along the coastal highway. "*I* can't wait to go snorkeling," she added eagerly.

"Swimming's fun," Bess countered with a shrug, "but eating lobster's definitely better."

From her seat beside George, Nancy turned toward her friends and smiled. "Can't you two agree on anything?" For as long as Nancy had known them, Bess and George had always seen things differently.

Even though George and Bess were cousins, they were contrasting opposites. George, dark haired and athletic, was always ready for a game or an adventure. Bess, blond, blue eyed, and slightly plump, preferred to avoid exercise or trouble whenever possible.

"Anyway," Nancy continued, "I know you both agree on how much you want to see Miss Braden."

"That's for sure," George said quickly. "She was the greatest elementary schoolteacher we ever had. I can't wait to see her!"

Bess leaned forward in her seat. "Neither can I," she said cheerfully. "But I still say we shouldn't pass up the chance to sample some great Down East seafood."

"I'm sure we'll have a chance to eat plenty of food and play tourist, too," said Nancy. She hesitated for a moment. "But you know, I can't help feeling that Miss Braden's invitation is something more than casual."

George shot a quick glance at Nancy. "Why do you say that?" she asked, then turned her attention back to the road.

"Because it's been ten years since Miss Braden left River Heights," Nancy replied. She leaned back in her seat. "Why does she want to see us now—out of the clear blue? It was a long time ago." Nancy closed her eyes. "I can see her clearly in my mind still,

2

though. Do you remember that baggy brown sweater she always wore?"

"I remember it!" Bess exclaimed. "The handmade one, with the white flowers on the front."

"Do you remember the nature walks Miss Braden was always taking us on?" George asked. "But she called them—"

"Observational tours," all three girls finished in unison, laughing.

Bess sat up straighter. " 'You must keep your eyes and your minds open,' " she said, trying to sound like their old teacher.

Nancy smiled. "She was always telling us that, wasn't she? Miss Braden made third grade so much fun."

"And anybody who could do that," George added, "had to be pretty special."

"We all had such a great time in her class," said Bess. "And then she moved away so suddenly. Do you remember why?"

"Her brother's wife became very ill, and Miss Braden moved to Maine to help him take care of his daughter. The little girl was only six, I think," Nancy said, jogging her friends' memories.

"I do remember now," Bess said sadly. "The girl's mother died a few months later."

For a moment the three girls were silent.

"I am glad Miss Braden wrote to Nancy," George said finally. "But it sure is strange hearing from her after all these years."

3

Nancy agreed. "Miss Braden sounded so cheerful in her letter. And she told me such wonderful things about her hometown and her family, but I can't help feeling there was something she wasn't saying."

"Do you think she has some kind of mystery for you to solve?" Bess turned to Nancy.

"I don't know how she'd know I was a detective," Nancy replied thoughtfully. She curled a strand of hair around her finger. "Miss Braden mentioned in her letter that her brother, Karl, was killed six months ago."

George shook her head. "I really feel sorry for the little girl. First her mother, then her father."

"Miss Braden said that her niece—whose name is Laura, I think—and her father were pretty close," said Nancy.

Bess placed a hand on Nancy's shoulder. "Sounds like you and your dad."

Nancy turned to give her friend a faint smile. Bess was right, she thought. Since her own mother had died, fifteen years before, Nancy and her father had become extremely close. She didn't know what she'd do if anything happened to him.

Nancy forced her thoughts back to Laura and Karl Braden. Miss Braden had written that six months earlier a terrible storm had struck. Karl's lobster boat had gone down, and he was lost at sea. Luckily, Laura hadn't been out lobstering with him that day.

"Maybe Miss Braden wants us to be company for

her niece," Bess offered. "You know, to help her get over all of this."

"Well, that would be strange, but I guess we'll learn more when we see her. In the meantime, let's just take in all this gorgeous scenery."

"Right," said George.

Nancy gazed out her window. The road they were on ran parallel to the New England coastline. Beyond the scattering of lush green trees, cream-colored sand, and the rocky, coal black shore lay the glittering waters of the Atlantic Ocean.

"To look at the ocean now, you wouldn't think it could ever be violent," Bess said.

Nancy knew exactly what her friends meant. Everything looked so picturesque and peaceful.

Small sailboats skimmed the surface of the water, and sea gulls floated on the gentle air currents of the perfect late-August sky.

Then the scenery began to change almost faster than the girls could take it in. They left the coast and were now looking at small houses and woodland areas, then at a scattering of small shops, gas stations, and roadside fruit stands.

Finally, this gave way to the ocean coastline again. Rows of cozy cottages and small houses were built along the water, many of them with docks. Some of the docks had small boats tied to them. Others were stacked high with fishing nets and old wooden lobster pots, cracked and worn gray by the sea.

The girls then entered the small coastal town that was their final destination.

"Let's find Miss Braden's house first," Nancy suggested. "She says it's just outside town. Then we can get something to eat." She pulled a letter from her purse. "According to the directions, Miss Braden lives near a naval base. And that one over there on the left must be it."

George slowed down as they drove past the entry gate for Stewart Naval Base. Except for the guard at the gate, the base didn't seem very impressive.

Five minutes later the girls were pulling into a driveway next to a small, salmon-colored house.

As they were mounting the steps of the front porch, the door swung open and a woman rushed out to greet them.

"Nancy, Bess, George!" she cried. "I'm so happy to see you!"

Nancy was amazed. Miss June Braden had hardly changed at all in the last ten years. Her reddish brown hair was now silvery gray, but otherwise she looked exactly the same. Short and wiry, with twinkling brown eyes and a small pointy nose, Miss Braden still seemed to have plenty of energy.

The teacher threw her arms around the girls in turn and hugged them as if they were her long-lost daughters.

"It's so good to see you all," she said. "And I've read and heard so much about your wonderful adven-

6

tures from my old friends and the River Heights paper." She quickly hugged Nancy again.

Nancy felt a warm glow as she returned the embrace. "We're glad to see you, too, Miss Braden." She grinned. "You were a strong influence on me, you know. 'See everything,' you always said. 'You never know when it might be useful.' That was a rule I learned well and use to this day."

Miss Braden looked pleased. She stepped back and studied the girls closely. "My, how all of you have grown. And you've become such attractive young ladies."

"It's been ten years, Miss Braden," Nancy replied, feeling a little embarrassed. "I guess we have grown a little."

The schoolteacher bent down and grabbed one of their bags. "Come on inside now. I've spent the past two hours preparing food for you."

"Great!" Bess exclaimed, then cleared her throat. "I mean—what a nice thing to do."

Nancy and George chuckled as they picked up their bags and followed Miss Braden into the house.

A short time later they were all sitting in the cozy kitchen, eating hot clam chowder and fresh-baked bread.

"I do hope you like that chowder," said Miss Braden. "There's plenty more." She smiled, but Nancy noticed that her eyes were full of sadness.

The teacher sighed. "I suppose I should explain

why I suddenly invited you all here. Before Laura comes home, I mean." She poured a cup of tea and took a sip of it, then she stared into the cup.

"Does it have anything to do with her father's death?" Nancy asked gently.

Miss Braden nodded. "Yes, it does. Karl's death was, of course, very tragic."

The three girls exchanged glances but said nothing.

"His boat, the *Lady Love*, went down a few miles off the coast of a cove nearby, Craven Cove," Miss Braden continued. "The sad thing is, he was actually quite close to a lighthouse and safety."

"He didn't see the lighthouse beacon?" Bess asked in surprise.

"No one will ever know for certain," Miss Braden answered. "But the reports claimed that the light was out and the storm made the sea pitch dark."

"How terrible," Bess said.

"Karl was a good sailor," Miss Braden went on. "We didn't know why he was out so late. He should have known better. Oh, that's right—you didn't know he was in the navy."

George seemed puzzled. "I thought he made his living as a lobsterman."

"Oh dear, no." Miss Braden smiled as if she was about to reveal some humorous secret. "Very few people can make a living lobstering. Karl was a naval engineer. He worked at the base."

8

"You mean the one right here in town?" Nancy asked.

"That's right," Miss Braden replied. "My brother was a very busy man. Sometimes he had to go to sea for weeks, but he always found time for Laura when he was at home. They were very close." She paused for a moment. "It took Laura a long time to accept his death," she continued. "Or at least I *thought* she had accepted it, until—"

Nancy sat upright in her chair. "What happened?" she asked.

Miss Braden sighed. "Laura has started going to Craven Cove at all hours of the day and night." She took another sip of tea. "Then, quite recently, she started saying—"

Nancy waited for Miss Braden to go on with her story, but the teacher seemed unable to finish.

"Please continue," Nancy urged gently.

"I don't know how to say this, Nancy," Miss Braden said slowly.

"Go on, Auntie," an angry voice interrupted.

Everyone turned toward the entrance to the kitchen. A raven-haired teenage girl stood in the doorway, her fists clenched at her side. Laura Braden, Nancy knew immediately.

Nancy could see the anger in the girl's clear gray eyes. Anger and fear.

"I said, go on and tell them," Laura repeated. "Tell them the whole story so they'll believe what

9

you and the entire town have decided—that I'm crazy!"

June Braden rose from her chair. "Now, Laura, you know I don't believe that."

"Sure you do!" Laura exploded. "And you're probably right. How else do you explain that twice in the past three weeks I've seen my father? I've seen a man who's supposed to be dead!"

2

Death at Sea

At first there was only silence in the kitchen.

Nancy found her voice first. "Maybe it was someone who looked like your father," she said.

"No, it wasn't," Laura Braden answered stubbornly. She moved quickly to the table and stood between Nancy and her aunt. "It's not just that I think I've seen him. It's more than that."

"What do you mean?" asked Nancy.

"I don't believe my father is dead," Laura said with determination. "I mean, I don't *feel* that he's really dead. My father and I were very close. If he were dead, I'd know it in my heart." Laura's eyes searched Nancy's. "He's alive, I know he is. And I want you to help me find him."

For a moment Nancy was speechless. She glanced quickly around the table at her friends. Bess and George looked skeptical. Nancy could tell from their faces that they felt sorry for Laura, but they didn't know what to think of her story.

Miss Braden simply looked worried. Whatever she thought about her niece's statement, she was keeping it to herself.

"That's why I asked Aunt June to send for you," Laura continued. "She's always read me clippings from the River Heights papers. A lot of them were stories about all the mysteries you've solved. I was sure that if anyone could help me, it would be Nancy Drew."

"Help you to do what?" Nancy asked.

"To find my father," Laura replied. "To prove he's alive."

Miss Braden reached for Laura's hand and squeezed it gently. "I told Laura not to expect too much," she said, glancing around the table. "After all, the police, the Coast Guard, and the naval authorities have closed their files already."

"But they think my father is dead," Laura argued. "I'm sure he isn't. And I need Nancy's help to prove it."

"But, Laura," George said gently, "if your father is alive, wouldn't he have come home by now?"

"Or at least called you," Bess added.

Laura Braden rubbed her forehead. "Maybe he's got amnesia," she said. "Maybe he can't remember where he lives or who he is." She looked from one face to another and then turned back to Nancy. "Look, if it wasn't my father, then who—or what—*did* I see? Please, Nancy, you've got to help me."

"This isn't my usual type of case," Nancy said, feeling awkward. "No actual crime has been committed, and all of the clues to the tragedy"—she searched for the right words—"were lost at sea."

Laura walked over to the kitchen window and stared outside for a moment. Then she took a deep breath and turned back to the others. "I know it sounds weird," she said. "Maybe it is just wishful thinking, but would you please help me, anyway?"

"I don't know what I could do," said Nancy. "I don't know this area very well—"

"Will you at least try?" Laura pleaded.

"Why don't you let me think about it a little, and then we'll talk some more." Nancy stood up and walked over to Laura. "I promise I'll give you an answer this evening."

Laura smiled. "Thanks," she said, her eyes shining.

"Don't thank me yet," said Nancy. "I haven't done anything."

"Is there anything I can do for you?" Laura asked.

"Well, sure," Nancy said with a grin. "Why don't you show me and my friends around town?"

"No problem," said Laura. "That'll be fun."

"Then it's settled." Miss Braden rose from the table. "But first have another helping of chowder—then your tour."

13

While Laura got out a bowl for herself and Miss Braden served the others, Nancy thought about Laura's problem.

The girl really believed her father was alive, even though common sense and everyone else indicated otherwise.

Nancy watched Laura as she chatted easily with Bess and George. She didn't seem like the kind of girl who'd make up such a story. If Laura hadn't been imagining things, then who had she seen? A Karl Braden look-alike—or someone or something else? Nancy frowned. Maybe she should decide to help the girl. If her anxieties could be put to rest then maybe she could begin to heal.

Immediately after their meal, the girls unpacked their bags. Then Laura drove them across a huge drawbridge that spanned a river and crossed into town.

Nancy, Bess, and George fell in love with the charming town. Laura led them through its clean and winding streets. They window-shopped for hand-made dolls and jewelry and rummaged through antique clothing and furniture stores.

Passersby said hello, church bells tolled the hours, and Laura was truly happy and at peace showing off her hometown.

By four o'clock the girls were strolling through a park at the edge of town. A damp, cool breeze started to blow onshore, and overhead the clear sky had turned a light shade of pewter gray.

"This is Preston Park," Laura said cheerfully. "It's one of the most popular spots in town. It's only three blocks square, but we get a lot of use out of it. For instance, from July through August the town sponsors an outdoor musical right here." She pointed to a circular stage in the center of the park. "The show has everything: lights, costumes, and a cast of thousands." She grinned. "Well, twenty-five, at least."

"It sounds wonderful," said Nancy. "Too bad we missed it."

Laura looked around at the trees, the flowers, and the people strolling by.

"My father used to bring me to see the show every year," she said. "After the show, we'd walk over to the docks to look at the pleasure boats moored to the pier down there."

Nancy, Bess, and George followed Laura to a guardrail that separated the park from the large river they had crossed to get into town. Piers jutted out into the swiftly flowing water.

Laura pulled her jacket collar up around her neck. "This river flows down from the White Mountains," she said. "It feeds into the ocean."

"This is beautiful," said Nancy. She watched several sailboats bobbing in the water. To her right was the drawbridge that spanned the river, which emptied into the harbor right there.

"Ships use this river after they enter the harbor to get to the navy yard," Laura said.

Across the water, the girls could see a row of two-

and three-story buildings. Some appeared to be barracks, but others looked like factories.

"Is that the base over there?" asked Nancy.

"It sure is," Laura replied. "Stewart Naval Base is a key defense point for this part of the East Coast."

"Where are all the big ships?" Bess asked excitedly.

"Most of them are out to sea," Laura answered. "They only come into dry dock for repairs, maneuvers, and crew reassignments. Even the subs don't stay too long."

"Submarines?" George sounded genuinely surprised.

"Sure," said Laura. "At least two nuclear subs use this base as a home port. But we don't see much of them. Their movements are kept pretty hush-hush. You know—spies and all."

"You sure know a lot about the base," George said admiringly.

"I should," Laura responded, a sadness in her voice. "My father worked there for ten years."

Nancy saw the hurt in Laura's eyes and tried to change the subject. "I thought you said this pier right behind us was mainly for pleasure boats."

"It is," said Laura.

"Then what is that?" Nancy pointed to a large, weather-beaten lobster boat tied to one of the docks.

Laura chuckled. "That's Uncle Sam's boat," she said.

"Uncle Sam? You mean the government owns that thing?" Bess had a puzzled look on her face.

16

"No," Laura replied. "Uncle Sam's full name is Sam Beaumont. He and my father grew up together. They've been friends for so long that I call him uncle."

"Does he have a little white beard?" Bess teased.

"No, he doesn't," said Laura, crinkling up her nose at Bess. "He has bright gray eyes, dark brown hair, and he can be pretty crabby at times. But I love him anyway." Laura started walking toward a gate in the railing. "He's probably delivering his catch to Captain Dan's." She pointed to a seafood restaurant just under the bridge.

"Come on," she said cheerfully. "I'll introduce you to him."

Nancy, George, and Bess followed Laura through a low metal gate and down a steep wooden ramp. Then they moved along the pier, passing a number of fancy cabin cruisers and speedboats, until they reached Sam's.

Where it was left, the paint on the boat was white. The hull and trim were sea green. The boat had obviously seen a lot of use. Everywhere Nancy looked, paint was cracking and peeling.

The wheelhouse was simple and was large enough to hold only two people comfortably.

Almost every inch of the exposed deck area was covered with lobster traps.

"Does Sam set all those traps by himself?" Nancy asked.

"Yes, but not all at once," Laura replied.

17

"Lobstermen set a few traps in one area, then move on to another. Sometimes it's days before they get back to check their first traps."

Suddenly a tall, lean man came around the far side of the cabin. He was wearing an old sweatshirt and baggy black overalls.

Though Laura had told them that Sam Beaumont was in his thirties, he looked much older to Nancy.

His complexion was dark and rough, like worn leather. His hands were massive and covered with scratches and calluses.

"Hi, Uncle Sam," said Laura. She stepped on board to hug him warmly. "I'd like you to meet some friends of mine."

The man gave the girls a quick nod.

"Nancy Drew, this is my uncle, Sam Beaumont," said Laura.

"Pleased to meet you, Mr. Beaumont," Nancy said politely.

"And this is Bess Marvin and George Fayne," Laura continued. "They all used to be students of Aunt June's back in River Heights."

"Hi," said George. "It's nice to meet you."

"Did you catch any lobsters today?" Bess asked eagerly.

"Caught my fair share," Sam Beaumont replied dryly. He swung onto the dock easily and shook hands with the girls.

Nancy could feel the strength in his grip and the rough texture of his skin.

18

"Don't let this guy fool you," said Laura. "Next to my dad, he's the best lobsterman in town." She turned to Sam. "Nancy's going to help me find out what happened to my dad."

Sam Beaumont shifted his gaze from Laura to Nancy, then back to Laura. Gently, he took hold of the girl's shoulders. "Laura, it's best that you let things be. Your father is gone now. And that's all there is to it."

"I don't believe that," Laura said forcefully. "I've seen him since the accident."

"Then you've seen his ghost," Sam said quietly.

Laura quickly pulled away from her uncle. "That's not true," she shouted. "He's alive out there!"

Sam Beaumont tensed. "Karl's engine blew, the boat went down, and that's all there is to it," he said tightly.

Nancy could see the desperation in Laura's eyes. "My father was a good lobsterman, a terrific sailor," Laura argued. "He knew how to handle a boat in a storm!"

"Your father was a navy man, not a lobsterman," Sam Beaumont growled. "If Karl had quit the navy and stuck to lobsters, maybe he wouldn't have—"

Abruptly he stopped and looked around at the four girls. His mood seemed to soften.

"I'm sorry, Laura," he said. "I guess Karl's death affected me more than I thought." A faint smile crossed his lips. "He *was* a good lobsterman, no doubt about it, but I'm a better one."

For a moment Laura looked as if she might cry, but then she smiled and Karl gave her a rough hug.

"I'd still like to know what he was doing out after dark," Sam muttered to himself.

"Is that true?" Bess asked, trying to help lighten the mood. "Are you really the best?"

"Might be," Sam replied. "You like lobsters?"

"I sure do!" said Bess.

"And any other seafood she can get her hands on," added George.

Sam Beaumont waved the girls on board and led them to a stack of traps near the cabin. Then he reached down and pulled up two large buckets filled with lobsters.

"Take your pick," he said calmly, holding the buckets toward Bess.

"But they're alive," Bess protested. She stared at the wriggling tangle of blackened shells, feelers, and claws. "You don't want me to take one out, do you?"

"Well . . ." Sam Beaumont replied with a shrug, drawing the word out. "It's not likely they'll follow you home."

Bess shuddered and took two steps back. "If you don't mind," she told him squeamishly, "I'll wait until they're, uh, cooked."

"For once, I'm with Bess," said George, moving closer to her cousin.

Nancy chuckled. "Maybe we'll pass on dinner," she said. "But we'd love to look around your boat."

Sam put the buckets back down. "I guess that can

20

be arranged," he said. "But I have to get these critters over to Captain Dan's right now. Laura, can you show them around?"

"Sure." Laura began moving toward the front of the vessel. "Uncle Sam's boat is very similar to my dad's," she told the others. "And I knew that one inside out."

After Laura, Bess, and George entered the cabin, Sam Beaumont stepped in front of Nancy, blocking her entry.

"What makes Laura think you should look into her father's accident?" he asked in a husky whisper, scowling at Nancy.

"I've done a little investigating in my time," she replied calmly.

Sam raised his brows. "You've investigated dead men?"

"Laura doesn't believe her father is dead," Nancy answered. "What do you think, Mr. Beaumont?"

The lobsterman stepped closer to Nancy. "Karl Braden is gone," he said, his broad frame looming over her. "In time, Laura will get used to that fact. But she won't if people let her believe that she'll see him again." Beaumont's voice became deep, and he spoke each word slowly. "It's best to let things be, Miss Drew, for her sake—and for yours."

3

The Face in the Cave

With that, Sam Beaumont picked up his lobsters, climbed quickly onto the dock, and headed for the restaurant.

As she watched him go, Nancy had the distinct feeling that Laura's uncle had just gone out of his way to threaten her. And if he had, why? What was he trying to hide?

Laura Braden's case was beginning to interest Nancy a great deal.

The tour of the boat was fun, but brief. Nancy noticed that Laura became steadily quieter and quieter until finally, when they left the pier, Laura was silent. The girls bundled back into her car.

"Where to now?" asked George. "The way those

clouds are beginning to darken, I hope it's someplace inside."

"There's a joke about Maine weather, you know," Laura said. "If you don't like it now, wait a few minutes."

The other girls chuckled. "Storms *can* pop up pretty fast around here," Laura continued. "Very fast, in fact. But we're not going indoors yet. We're heading for Craven Cove."

"Are you sure you want to go there?" Nancy asked, concerned. "I know what it means to you, but—"

"Don't worry about that," said Laura. "The cove happens to be one of the prettiest places in this area. I'd be a lousy tour guide if I didn't show it to you."

"Are you sure?" asked Bess.

Laura smiled as she pressed down harder on the gas pedal. "I'm fine, really. I promise, it's a sight you won't want to miss."

Nancy and her friends exchanged quick glances, then settled back in their seats to admire the view.

For the next fifteen minutes, the car sped along a two-lane road that ran parallel to the coastline. Tall oaks towered overhead, occasionally giving way to large beachfront homes and boat houses.

Finally Laura turned onto a gravel-topped road and drove past a sign that read Craven Cove, One Mile.

Laura expertly guided the car along the narrow, bumpy trail. Nancy couldn't help but notice that Laura took the sharp turns as if she knew them well.

She wondered how often Miss Braden's niece had visited the cove since her father's accident.

Soon the trees vanished and the road stopped suddenly. Straight ahead lay a beautiful, sandy beach that ran down to the water, at least a hundred yards away. The beach stretched along the waterline about three miles in both directions.

Huge boulders jutted up out of the water, some of them blackened by seaweed and algae. Powerful waves crashed against the rocks, sending sprays of white foam leaping into the air.

To their left, above the beach, the girls saw several small houses and docks. A few boats bobbed in the water nearby.

To their right, the land gradually sloped upward into a steep, rocky cliff, its face pocked with small openings and ledges.

On either side of the cove, at the far ends of two stone jetties, were two old lighthouses, towering guardians of the peace and beauty of Craven Cove. It was a postcard-perfect blend of sand and sea.

The girls stepped out of the car.

"You were right," George said breathlessly. "This place is beautiful even on a cloudy day like this."

"Yes, it is," said Laura, nodding. "Now you know why I like to come here so much. Not only to feel closer to my father, but also because the cove is a great place to be alone and think."

"Where did your father have his accident?" Nancy

asked cautiously. She didn't want to bring up painful memories for Laura, but the girl had asked for her help.

"Just beyond the lighthouses," Laura replied. "A couple of miles out."

"Which one malfunctioned?" asked George.

"The one on the right." There was anger in Laura's voice. "It's operated by an elderly couple, the Gessups. The other lighthouse hasn't been used in years." Then she pointed to the cliff on their right. "We could get a better view of the cove from up there."

"Sounds good to me if it doesn't start raining," said Nancy, staring up at the gathering clouds that all but obliterated the sun now.

Bess gazed up at the steep face of the cliff and shook her head. "I can see just fine from down here. In fact," she said brightly, "I think I'll walk along the beach and collect shells."

"That's my cousin," George said with a laugh. "I'll keep Bess company for a while, then I'll catch up with you."

"Okay," said Nancy, hurrying after Laura.

The climb wasn't that difficult. Nancy found hand- and footholds easily. Before she knew it, she and Laura were standing on a ledge overlooking part of the cove.

The cliff still rose a good distance above them. Nancy glanced around and noticed a few feet away an opening that looked like the mouth of a small cave. A chain was stretched across the opening and a sign hanging from it was marked Danger.

"What's in there?" asked Nancy.

"Oh, that leads to tunnels in the cliff," Laura replied. "It used to be a smugglers' hideout. In fact, Craven Cove used to be called Smuggler's Cove."

Visions of pirates and princesses filled Nancy's mind as she gazed out over the cove.

"In the 1800s, there was a fort up there, on top of the cliff," Laura told her. "Soldiers used the tunnels as escape passages during bombardment. But no one goes in there now."

"Not that I'd want to," Nancy said with a grin, "but why not?"

Laura moved along the ledge toward the opening. "Mainly because the tunnels connect with an underground pool that's fed by the sea. At high tide the tunnels fill up with water and—"

Suddenly Laura's words caught in her throat. Nancy turned to see the young girl staring at the mouth of cave, frozen in terror.

Nancy could make out Laura's words under the roar of the sea.

"Daddy!" Laura screamed. "Daddy, come back!"

4

Laura's Story

"Daddy!" Laura screamed again, and started for the cave.

Nancy raced along the ledge. Bits and pieces of loose rock shifted under her feet, and twice she nearly lost her footing. Below her was a twenty-foot drop to the rocky shore.

Somehow she managed to keep her balance and leap over the chain to reach Laura just inside the cave entrance.

"Laura, don't!" Nancy shouted as she grabbed the girl.

"That was him! That was my father!" screamed Laura, trying to pull away. "You saw him, didn't you? You *had* to see him!"

"Actually," Nancy said, frowning, "I didn't see anything. I was too far away, but I believe he could have been there."

"But you must have seen him," Laura said, breaking free of Nancy's grip. "He was standing right there at the entrance!"

Nancy and Laura were standing and straining to see into the blackness. The cave wasn't much more than five feet high and four feet wide, but it looked like a tunnel that went on forever.

"I can't see a thing," Nancy said. She carefully walked a few feet into the semidarkness. The floor was littered with loose rocks, and Nancy tripped on one of them. She pitched forward and fell flat on her knees and hands.

"Are you all right?" Laura asked in alarm, hurrying over to Nancy.

"I'm fine," Nancy replied as she pushed herself up on her knees. She looked at her hands. Even in the dim light she could see that they were covered with black dirt. "I'll have a lot of fun trying to get this stuff off my clothes," she said, standing up and trying to dust herself off. "Let's talk more about this outside, okay?"

Reluctantly, Laura allowed Nancy to lead her back out onto the ridge.

"What happened?" called a concerned voice as the two girls emerged into steel gray light and a soft rain.

Nancy looked down to see George and Bess

scurrying up the rocks, raindrops dripping off their noses.

"Are you guys all right?" Bess asked breathlessly, wiping a hand across her face. "We heard a scream."

"And when we looked up, you disappeared among the rocks," George finished.

Bess looked down nervously at the narrow width of the ledge. "Tell me what happened quickly," she said, "before I realize where I am and faint."

"Laura saw someone in the cave," Nancy explained.

"Not just *someone*," Laura said quickly. "It was my father. I know it was."

"Did you see him?" George asked Nancy.

"No," Nancy replied cautiously. She put an arm around Laura's shoulders. "I couldn't see the entrance from where I was standing."

Laura appeared to be on the verge of tears. "You've got to believe me, Nancy. You've just got to."

Nancy didn't know what to say. She didn't believe that Laura could have seen her father, but she did think the girl had seen something. Something that had upset her terribly.

Also, Nancy couldn't stop thinking about Sam Beaumont. Had he really meant to threaten her? And if so, why?

"I believe something strange is going on," Nancy told Laura. "I don't know what it is or why it's happening to you. But I promise you I'll find out before we leave."

29

Laura looked relieved. She combed her hair with her fingers and gave the girls a faint smile.

"Excuse me," Bess said nervously, "but it's chilly and raining, and we're here standing on the edge of a cliff. Couldn't we find a better place to talk?"

"You're right," Nancy said. "In fact, I could use something hot to drink."

"There's a roadside diner not too far from here," said Laura. "We could go there."

"Sounds good to me," said George. "Let's go."

As it began to pour, the girls started their descent to the beach.

A few feet down the cliff Nancy wiped an arm across her face to sweep the wet strands of hair out of her eyes. She turned to look back at the cave. Maybe someone *had* been there. Someone who looked enough like Karl Braden to fool his own daughter. Someone who would rather run blindly into a dark tunnel than be seen up close.

Laura was convinced that her father was alive, but why, Nancy asked herself, would Karl Braden pretend to be dead?

Nancy was intrigued. There definitely was a mystery at Craven Cove—and one that might pose a threat to Laura Braden.

Nancy made a promise to herself. For Laura's sake, and for Miss Braden's, she would find out what was going on. Then Laura would know for sure if her father was alive or dead.

* * *

The Back Bay Diner, about three miles from the cove, was warm and dry. The girls found a comfortable booth in the corner and ordered cocoa.

Outside, the rain beat wildly against the windows. "We may need a boat to get back to your house, Laura," Bess joked.

"This probably won't last long," said Laura. She gazed out the window, watching the tree branches whipping in the wind. Small streams were forming along the road. "This is nothing compared to the storm that sank my father's boat."

"If you can," Nancy said, "tell us about the accident."

Laura continued to stare out the window. "The radio had been broadcasting storm warnings all that day," she began quietly. "But my dad insisted on taking the boat out."

"He wasn't worried about the storm?" Bess asked.

"No," Laura replied, "but I think something else was bothering him."

Nancy raised her brows. "Did you ask him what it was?"

"No," Laura answered. "I figured it was probably navy business. Sometimes he had to solve a communications problem on a ship or submarine. And he couldn't talk about those sorts of things."

"Top secret?" asked George.

"Top-top hush-hush," Laura said with a faint smile.

The waitress brought their drinks, then walked back to the counter.

"Mmm, this is yummy," said Bess, taking another sip of her cocoa. "I'm starting to feel warm all over."

Nancy dipped a spoon in her cup to sample the whipped cream floating on top. "Go on with your story, please," she said.

"Well," Laura said slowly, "Dad took the boat out around four o'clock, which was unusual since it was already getting dark. I tried to warn him about the storm, but he wouldn't listen. He wouldn't let me go with him, either. The storm front hit about seven, and the thunder was so loud I could feel it booming inside me."

"Your father didn't start heading back to shore when he saw all of that?" Nancy asked in surprise.

Laura gripped her cup tightly. "We don't know." She paused for a moment. "The storm lasted a couple of hours. As soon as it was over, Aunt June and I went to the docks."

A single tear ran down Laura's cheek.

"He never came home," she said in a trembling voice. "Search parties went looking for him, and the next morning they found only the wreckage of his boat."

Nancy frowned. "Wreckage? You mean his boat didn't just sink?"

Laura shook her head. "It was totally smashed to pieces. The Coast Guard figured that the boat must have struck rocks. They searched for Dad and so did some of his friends, like Uncle Sam. Even the navy sent out boats. Their search was led by Commander Daindridge."

"Who is he?" Nancy asked.

"He was my father's commanding officer at the base," Laura replied. "He was also one of Dad's closest friends. Commander Daindridge insisted on leading the search."

"But?" Nancy left her question unfinished.

"He finally gave up, too," Laura continued. The case was closed and my father was officially listed as missing at sea."

Suddenly Laura grew agitated. "Don't you see?" she asked. "They never found him. All those people and equipment, and they didn't find him. That means he could have survived, right? The man I saw at the cove could really have been my father!"

Nancy didn't reply. Something about Laura's story sparked an idea. Where was the body? She knew one thing for certain: she needed more information.

"It's too late tonight. Tomorrow I'll do some checking with the Coast Guard and the naval base," Nancy said finally. "I don't know what I'll find out, but—"

"If there's anything to be found," Bess said proudly, "Nancy will find it."

"Thanks for the vote of confidence," Nancy teased.

Laura let out a deep sigh of relief. "I'm so glad you're working on this, Nancy. I know you'll find my father."

"All I can do is promise to try my best," Nancy said.

33

"In the meantime, I think it would be best if we didn't talk to anybody else about this—at least, not until we have more facts."

"Whatever you say," Laura answered. She looked out the window again. The rain was only a drizzle now and the wind had died down.

"I told you the storm wouldn't last long," she said cheerfully. "Let's go home. We can change out of these soggy clothes and build a fire in the fireplace."

"Sounds great to me," Bess said.

Just as the girls reached the cash register, a very well dressed woman approached them. Her hair was dark brown and cut short in a no-nonsense style. She had small ferret eyes, thin lips, and a very large nose.

"Laura Braden," the woman greeted her. "I was just thinking about you."

Nancy glanced from the woman to Laura. Miss Braden's niece didn't look happy to see this woman.

"Hi, Ms. Walters," Laura said coolly. "I haven't seen you since right after my father's accident."

"Aren't you going to introduce me to your friends?" Without waiting for an answer, Ms. Walters extended her hand to Nancy. "Anne Marie Walters," she said with an exaggerated air of importance. "I'm a reporter with the *Herald*, the local paper. In fact, I'm one of the best reporters they have," she added with a laugh, trying to tone down her obvious bragging.

"Ms. Walters wrote the story about my father's disappearance." Nancy noticed that Laura was sounding more and more annoyed.

"It was a good piece, too, sweetheart," said the reporter. "Even though you weren't very cooperative."

"You wouldn't leave me and my aunt alone," Laura said angrily. "You kept asking all those questions about the accident, my father's work at the naval base, my mother's death! You even hinted in your story that my father might have had something to hide."

A smirk appeared on the reporter's face. "Why else would Karl Braden go out on a night when no sane sailor would dare to?"

"Well, I'm sure he had a good reason," Nancy broke in. She was beginning to dislike the reporter now, too.

"All I know, sweetheart," said Ms. Walters, "is that a naval radio engineer went out late on a February day on a small lobster boat, despite an approaching storm. The storm struck, a lighthouse malfunctioned, and the boat was destroyed. The head of base security led the search for him—"

"Captain Daindridge was my father's friend," Laura said loudly. "That's why he led that search."

The reporter seemed unmoved by Laura's outburst. "That's what you say, but as we all know, there was a lot of smuggling going on around here then. My nose for news told me this story is connected."

"With a nose like that," Bess whispered to George, "I'm surprised it's not shouting to her."

George nodded in agreement.

"What are you getting at?" Nancy asked Anne Marie Walters.

The reporter looked down her nose at the girls for a moment before answering. "I'm not 'getting at' anything. I'm stating that I think Karl Braden was involved in smuggling and that there was a big cover-up surrounding his death. I've been working for six months to get the proof I need to expose Karl Braden for the thief he was."

5

A Nose for News

"Ms. Walters," Nancy said, "why are you so sure something's being covered up?"

"Why did Braden sail out into a storm, and why did the head of naval security lead the search for him personally? I've already been over this, sweetheart," Ms. Walters replied.

Nancy frowned. "My name is Nancy, Ms. Walters. Nancy Drew."

"Drew? Nancy Drew?" the reporter repeated. She seemed to be thinking, then suddenly her eyes opened wide and she smiled crookedly. "Of course! I've read about you. You're the girl who goes around playing detective. Don't tell me you're investigating Karl Braden's death?"

"I'm here visiting friends," Nancy replied.

"Let me guess. Your friends wouldn't just happen to be the Bradens?" Ms. Walters asked. Her eyes narrowed. "I wasn't born yesterday," she said. "Whatever you're up to, I'll find out eventually anyway. So why don't you level with me now?"

Nancy stepped around the reporter and approached the lady at the cash register. "My friends and I are simply here on vacation," she said. Nancy handed the check and money to the cashier.

"Of course you are, dear." Ms. Walters reached into her purse and pulled out a business card. "If you decide you have something to tell me, give me a call." She pressed the card into Laura's hand and crossed the room to sit in the booth the girls had just left.

"I'm not surprised she's eating alone," George whispered to the others.

"She makes me so angry," Laura said, crumpling the card in her hand. "How dare she suspect my father of anything wrong!"

"She's certainly not the nicest person I've ever met," Bess said.

"She's certainly not the most professional reporter, either," said George. "At least she's still looking into your father's case. Maybe she'll actually find something."

"Sure," Laura said bitterly. "Something that'll blacken my father's name."

"She can't find anything that's not there," said Nancy, collecting her change and starting for the

38

door. "Let's go home, gang. That warm fireplace still sounds good to me. And tomorrow we can start searching for ourselves."

The next day Nancy woke up smiling. Her room was on the top floor of the Bradens' house, and sunlight filtered in around the shade, warming the room with soft peach tones. The aroma of waffles cooking drifted up the stairs and tugged at Nancy to get out of bed.

Nancy didn't want to budge yet, though. She was much too comfortable beneath the sheets and the thick, handmade quilt.

Soon memories of the events of the day before rushed into her mind, crowding out all thoughts of lingering in bed.

Laura was certain she had seen her father at Craven Cove, but Nancy hadn't seen anyone.

Nancy remembered how Sam Beaumont had warned her to stop her investigation when he found out she was looking into Braden's disappearance. Then there had been Ms. Walters. Was she just a rude, aggressive reporter making wild guesses, or did she have the facts to back up her accusations?

Nancy had a lot of questions to answer, and she wouldn't find any answers in bed, she knew. She threw back the covers in one movement and rose to face the day.

After a delicious breakfast, Nancy and the others looked at a set of news clippings that Laura had saved about her father's accident. She had kept them, hoping to find some clue to her father's whereabouts.

Meanwhile, Miss Braden went up to the attic and returned with a cardboard storage box. It was filled with Karl Braden's letters, business papers, and some of his navy records.

"What's this?" Nancy asked, picking up an old brown book.

Miss Braden chuckled. "That's Karl's old code book. He got it when he was a boy. It was always one of his favorite things."

Nancy placed the book, Karl Braden's papers, and all the clippings on the table in neat piles. Then the others gathered around and started to look through them.

"I've read these over and over again," Laura said, holding up a handful of newspaper articles. "I hope you can find something I couldn't, Nancy."

"I hope so, too," Nancy said. She looked over at Miss Braden and smiled. " 'See everything—you never know when you might need it.' "

Miss Braden returned the smile. Then her face grew sad as she looked at an old photograph of her brother. "He was so handsome," she said with a sigh. Miss Braden passed a photo to Nancy, and Bess and George peered over her shoulder.

Nancy looked at the snapshot carefully. Karl Braden was standing proud and tall in his navy uniform. His white hat was tipped to one side, and a large duffel bag was leaning against his leg.

"He looks very young in this photo," said Nancy. "When was this taken?"

"Just before he shipped out overseas, I believe," Miss Braden replied. "He was eighteen, and so pleased with himself. He'd not only made it into the navy, but they were going to give him special training."

"In engineering?" Nancy asked.

"That's right," said Miss Braden. "Karl loved working on all kinds of electronic equipment. When he was a boy, he used to have a shortwave radio. He spent hours sending coded messages to his friends."

"So, he joined the navy and went overseas," Nancy said thoughtfully.

Miss Braden held up several bundles of envelopes tied with faded blue ribbons. "He wrote a great deal—especially to Donna."

"That was my mother," Laura put in.

"They dated all through high school," Miss Braden continued. "Anyway, Karl stayed overseas for two years. Then he came home, married Donna, and continued his training. He shipped out a few more times, but finally he was assigned to the base here."

"I was born a year later," Laura added.

"After Donna died, Karl's life was Laura and the navy," said Miss Braden.

"But he did find time to go lobstering," Bess said.

"He only started that the past few years," said Laura. "Uncle Sam talked Dad into it. He told Dad he needed a relaxing hobby."

41

Nancy frowned, looking up from the papers. "Well, so far I haven't found anything that might help us. But maybe we should find out more about what the search for him turned up. Do you think your father's commanding officer will talk to us?"

"Commander Daindridge?" Laura asked. "Probably. I see him once in a while. He likes to eat at the restaurant where I work part-time. And he lives nearby. I'll give him a call."

Laura ran into the kitchen and called the base. Within a few minutes she had spoken to the commander and returned to the table.

"The commander said he's very busy, but he'd be able to see us for a few minutes," Laura said.

"Great," said Nancy. "Let's go."

Miss Braden began to put the papers away. "You girls go ahead," she said. "I have some errands to run in town. School starts in another week and I have things to prepare. I'll see you all later."

"Okay," said Nancy. She and the others grabbed their jackets and hurried out the door.

It was only a five-minute drive to Stewart Naval Base. The guard told the girls that he had just been given their names by Commander Daindridge. He allowed them to pass through the gate.

Laura drove along a paved road that wound around a number of large buildings.

"The big white buildings are barracks, and the tall gray ones are the warehouses, motor pools, and work areas," she explained.

"Where is Commander Daindridge's office?" Bess asked.

"Over there," said Laura, pointing to a redbrick building just ahead. Although the building was only one story tall, it was about a block long. There were iron bars on all the windows.

George leaned forward in her seat to get a better look. "Is the commander a spy?"

"Commander Daindridge is in charge of naval base security," said Laura. "He and my dad worked mostly on air wave security. You know, scrambling and unscrambling radio messages from Washington, navy ships, and—"

"Submarines," Bess added. "Like the ones that patrol the coastline."

"That's right," said Laura. She pulled the car into a parking space just in front of the building. "We're here."

Just inside the building a guard was seated at a desk. He led them down a narrow corridor to a door bearing the commander's name. He took them inside, saluted the commander, and left the room.

The commander came out from behind his desk with his hand extended. "I'm glad to see you, Laura." He took her hand and squeezed it gently. "How are you?"

"I'm just great, Commander Daindridge," Laura replied. "Especially now." She looked quickly at Nancy.

Commander Daindridge was not tall, but he was

built like a big man, with broad shoulders. His movements were sharp and quick, and Nancy had the feeling he'd be a dangerous opponent in a fight.

"Aren't you going to introduce me to your friends?" the commander asked Laura. He flashed each of the girls a dazzling smile.

After Laura introduced them, the commander gestured for everyone to sit down.

"As I told you, Laura," he said, "I have only a few minutes to spare."

"We know, sir," Nancy spoke up, deliberately interrupting Laura. She was afraid that Laura would tell the commander she was a detective, and she didn't want any more people knowing. "We're here visiting Miss Braden," she said.

"She used to be our elementary-school teacher, back in River Heights," added Bess, eager to be part of the conversation.

"That's nice," said the commander. He flashed Bess another winning smile, and she beamed.

"Laura told us about her father's accident," Nancy continued. "She's still very upset about it, and I thought talking to you might help her and us understand exactly what your search turned up."

The commander didn't reply immediately. He seemed to be weighing his words carefully.

He leaned back in his chair, folded his arms across his chest, and stared silently at each girl in turn.

After a moment or two he spoke. "Laura," he said, looking right at her, "I know your father's death has been hard on you. I know it has been hard for you to accept, but you must. Your father's boat went down, and I'm afraid he went down with it."

"You found the boat, didn't you?" Bess asked.

"We found wreckage," the commander replied, eyeing her carefully. "Bits and pieces, but we didn't find the whole boat."

"You never found Karl Braden's body, did you?" Nancy asked.

"No, we didn't," Commander Daindridge replied. "But that's not unusual. The ocean is a very big place, and that storm was a strong force. The body could have been carried anyplace."

"Do you know why the lighthouse didn't work that night?" George asked.

The commander leaned forward on his desk, folded his hands, and looked George straight in the eye. "I believe there was a circuit failure in the main generator."

"But doesn't the lighthouse have a backup generator, in case of emergencies?" Nancy asked.

"Yes, it does," the naval officer replied, fixing his concentration straight on her. "That generator burned out, too, though. Unfortunately, these things can happen."

Commander Daindridge pressed a button on his intercom, then stood up and came around to the front of the desk. "I'm afraid I've run out of time, ladies."

"Thank you for seeing us," Nancy said, extending her hand.

45

"You're perfectly welcome," the commander replied. "I hope I was of some help." He turned to Laura. "You take care of yourself now."

"I will," she told him.

A navy ensign waited at the door and led the girls back to the front of the building.

Once outside, George turned to Nancy. "Well, that was a waste of time," she said. Then she and Bess climbed into the back of Laura's car.

"Oh, I don't know about that," Nancy replied. She stood looking at the building for a few seconds before slipping into the front passenger seat. "The whole time we were with the commander," Nancy said, "I had the feeling I was a bug under a microscope. He was very careful about everything he said."

"You sound like that reporter," Bess teased.

"But don't forget," Laura said, "Commander Daindridge was a friend of my father's. I've known him almost my entire life. He'd tell me if he knew anything."

"Maybe," Nancy replied. But she wasn't convinced.

"Well," Laura said, "what's our next move?"

"I don't know yet," Nancy answered. She took a deep breath and the salty sea air caused her body to tingle. "But while I'm thinking about it, why don't we explore the area?"

The rest of the day was devoted to fun. The girls shopped for a couple of hours in a nearby town, then went to have lunch at a restaurant called the Bread and Bowl.

Laura led them through the reproduction Colonial tavern out to a table on the back porch. There they ate their lunch beside a small brook. The water flowed gently over the rocks and poured down to form a small waterfall.

It was heaven.

That evening during dinner Miss Braden was happy to hear about their outing. "I'm so glad you had some fun," she said. "I was afraid you'd spend your whole vacation, well—"

"Chasing ghosts?" Laura asked sarcastically.

"In a way, Laura," Miss Braden replied kindly. "You do have to prepare yourself for the possibility that your father—"

"My father is *alive!*" Laura insisted. "He may be hurt out there, and I'm the only one who seems to care!"

Miss Braden seemed stunned by her niece's outburst. "Laura, that's simply not true. I loved my brother."

"I'm sorry, Aunt June." Laura ran over and gave Miss Braden a hug.

"It's okay, sweetheart," said Miss Braden. She held Laura close to her. "It's hard for me, too."

"Excuse me," Laura said. She pulled away from her aunt and glanced at Nancy and her friends. "I think I'll go to my room."

"Would you like someone to talk to?" Nancy asked.

Laura shook her head. "No, thanks. I think I'd like to be alone for a while." She ran quickly out of the kitchen and up the stairs.

"I really appreciate all you're doing, girls," Miss Braden said softly.

"I know how I'd feel if anything happened to my parents," Bess said.

"Me, too," George agreed. "My family is very close."

"I remember your parents," Miss Braden told Bess and George. "And I remember your father, Nancy." The schoolteacher seemed lost in her thoughts.

Then Nancy, Bess, and George watched as their ex-teacher's eyes grew wide. They followed her gaze and saw Laura standing in the doorway.

The girl looked terrified. Her skin was pale and she seemed to be having trouble breathing.

In her outstretched hand was a length of sailing cord dangling from her index finger. A cold chill went through Nancy's body as she saw that the rope was tied in a series of knots.

And the knots ended in a hangman's noose!

6

The Night Visitor

Nancy and George rushed over to help Laura into a chair at the table. Bess placed a sweater around the girl's trembling shoulders, and Laura's aunt poured her a cup of hot tea.

"Laura," Nancy said after the girl had calmed down a bit, "tell us what happened."

"When I walked into my room I found this." Laura placed the rope on the table. "It was wedged in my window, which I'd left partially open to get some fresh air."

Nancy carefully picked up the nylon cord. She was relieved to discover that it wasn't a noose after all. The rope was actually a series of complicated twists and knots that formed a loop.

"Lots of fishermen and lobstermen use these

knots," said Laura, beginning to seem a little calmer. "But this isn't just *any* rope," she continued. "This was a gift. My father gave it to me when I was a little girl. He must have left it for me to tell me he's still alive." Laura took a sip of tea as a shiver went through her body.

"But how did he get it and stick it in your window?" Miss Braden asked.

"I don't know," Laura answered. "It's been in a box in my closet for years. I saw the rope in its box just last week."

Nancy frowned. Could it be possible that Laura wasn't telling them the truth?

"Everybody wait here," she ordered, heading for the kitchen door. "I'm going to take a look around outside."

"Do you want some help?" asked George.

"No, thanks," Nancy replied. "It's pretty dark and muddy out there. If there are any clues, they'll be easier to find if there aren't too many people walking around."

"There's a flashlight in the hall closet," Miss Braden called after her. "Be careful!"

Nancy grabbed her jacket and the flashlight and raced outside.

A fine rain was falling as Nancy stepped out onto the porch. She could feel the cold water against her face and down her neck.

She pulled her jacket close about her, turned on the flashlight, and walked carefully around to the back of the house. While she went she tried to decide if Laura was lying. Could she have made up the whole story?

The night was dark. Even though there were two street lamps not far from the house, they didn't throw much light. Nancy saw only misty black shapes and silhouettes.

Nancy swept her flashlight beam in front of her as she walked, but the light was swallowed up by the thin fog that swiveled close to the ground.

At first she didn't see anything, but then she spotted them—a trail of footprints in the earth just below Laura's window.

Nancy moved the beam of light up the side of the house. A vine-covered trellis led all the way to the top floor. There were muddy smudges where someone had touched the trellis climbing up to Laura's room.

Nancy knelt to examine the footprints. She noticed that the tips of the large shoes were rounded, and the soles were made up of a series of crisscross grooves.

She committed the design to memory before rising to follow the tracks to a low hedge at the end of Miss Braden's property.

Beyond the hedge lay several acres of woods: a mass of tangled branches and deep, black shadows.

Nancy stepped carefully over the hedge and followed the prints for a few feet. The ground was covered with wet leaves and broken twigs, and the footprints soon vanished abruptly.

She flashed her light all around. The trees before

her seemed to press together like an angry crowd, and overhead their branches and leaves formed a dark canopy. Nancy couldn't help but feel that the woods were closing in on her.

She'd never find anyone in there, Nancy knew. Laura's unknown visitor had gotten away for now.

She made one more sweep of the backyard, then returned to the house.

"Did you find anything?" Miss Braden asked anxiously as Nancy entered the kitchen.

"Yes, I did," Nancy replied. She told the others about the muddy smudges on the trellis and described the footprints she had discovered.

"These prints sound like they were made by fisherman's shoes," Miss Braden said. "The soles are deeply grooved to give them better traction on a wet boat deck."

"A lobsterman would wear shoes like that," Laura said excitedly. "See, I told you my father is alive. He left the rope as some kind of message."

"Maybe," Nancy said. "But if he *is* alive, why is he hiding?"

"And if he wants everyone to think he's dead," George added, "why would he leave this rope?"

"This is getting a little spooky for me," said Bess. "I mean, if a ghost isn't doing this, then there's a real weirdo running around here."

"I'm almost sorry I asked you girls to come," said Miss Braden, pursing her lips. "This is all very strange, and I don't want anything to happen to any of you."

"I don't think we're in any danger," Nancy reassured her. "But I have to admit, a lot of strange things have been happening. Laura's father may have been involved in something that—"

"My father is not a crook!" Laura shouted.

"I didn't say he was," Nancy said quickly. "But if he *is* alive, then for some reason he's afraid to show himself. He needs our help. But we can't do anything until we discover what he was up to before his accident."

Nancy moved over to the window and stared out into the rainy darkness. Against the sky the lights from the naval base cast a pale yellow haze. "The answers are out there," she said. "And tomorrow, we're going to find them."

Late the next morning Nancy, Bess, and George drove Laura to the Fair Weather Inn, a restaurant in the center of town.

"Eleven fifty-five," said George, glancing at her watch as Laura pushed open the car door. "You just made it."

"It's my fault we ran late," said Laura. She quickly grabbed a canvas bag from the back seat that contained her apron and shoes. "I didn't sleep very well last night, and I feel a little weird."

"You'll be fine as soon as you start your shift," said

Nancy. She helped Laura pull her bike out of the trunk. "Are you sure you don't want us to pick you up?"

"I'm sure," Laura answered. "I only work the lunch-hour shift, Wednesday through Friday. I should be finished by three o'clock. I'll ride home and meet you guys there."

With a wave, Laura Braden hurried into the restaurant.

"Why isn't she driving her car?" asked George.

"She said parking in town in the summer is hard, and she can make almost as fast time on her bike," Nancy explained.

"I sure feel sorry for her," said Bess from the back seat. "She's trying so hard to cope with everything.

"I know what you mean," said George. "I sure hope we can help her."

"I hope so, too," said Nancy almost to herself. She swung the car around and headed down a narrow street.

"Where are we going?" Bess asked. "It is lunchtime."

"Well, then, I guess we'll have to stop for lunch," Nancy replied. "But later, I want to pay a call on a certain reporter."

George frowned. "I may skip that visit. I didn't like Ms. Walters much."

Nancy chuckled. She knew exactly what George meant. But they had to talk to the woman. Nancy remembered that the reporter had mentioned smuggling in connection with the Braden case, and Nancy wanted to know why.

The girls had lunch in the restaurant of an old hotel. The four-story mansion sat on the water's edge, overlooking most of the town. It was surrounded by large weeping willows, well-tended flower gardens, and clipped hedges.

Through the restaurant window the girls could see the twin lighthouses that marked the entrance to Craven Cove.

"One lighthouse has been abandoned for years," said Nancy thoughtfully. "And the other is run by an elderly couple."

"And that one happened to break down," Bess said, wiping a bit of apple cobbler from her lips, "the very night Karl Braden needed it."

"What do you think could make both generators go out at the same time?" asked George.

"I don't know," said Nancy slowly. "That's one more thing to find out."

Nancy brought Bess and George back to Miss Braden's house around two. The cousins wanted to spend some time with their old teacher, so Nancy decided to visit Ms. Walters alone.

She arrived at the *Herald* office half an hour later. She had no trouble locating the reporter.

The *Herald* newsroom was a large open space with four or five desks placed in the center of the room. Nancy noticed a series of private work spaces along the far wall, separated by dividers. The dividers, about five feet high, created a line of miniature offices.

"You want to see Anne Marie?" asked one of the busy workers, looking up from her desk. The small name tag she was wearing read Thomasina. "You'll find her ladyship in that cubicle on the end."

"Thank you," Nancy said.

"I'll see if you still want to thank me after you've met her," said the woman. She returned to her work.

Nancy knocked and entered the makeshift office. Anne Marie Walters was sitting at her desk. The walls of her cubicle were lined with clippings of various stories she had written—all of them framed.

The reporter looked up from her computer. "Well, if it isn't little Miss Drew," she said. "Don't tell me you've come to share secrets."

Nancy took a deep breath and let it out slowly. "I've come to ask you about Karl Braden," she said.

Ms. Walters raised an eyebrow. "I thought you said you weren't investigating the Braden case."

"The things you said yesterday got Laura pretty upset," Nancy replied. "I'd like to find out why you believe her father was doing something illegal."

She leaned back in her chair with a smile. "Well, it doesn't work like that, honey—uh, Ms. Drew. If you want information, you have to give some in return."

"I don't know anything at the moment," said Nancy. "Except that Laura Braden believes her father is alive." Nancy was careful not to reveal anything that the whole town didn't already know.

"Old news," Ms. Walters replied with a shrug. "Look, young lady, Karl Braden was definitely up to something just before he disappeared."

"And do you know what he was doing?" Nancy asked.

Ms. Walters smiled her crooked smile. "I'm not saying I do, and I'm not saying I don't."

"Then you're not saying very much, Ms. Walters," Nancy answered evenly.

"That's true," the reporter admitted. "But if you really want to know what I know, you can read my column."

"Then I guess we have nothing more to discuss." Nancy stood and started across the newsroom.

By the time she reached her car, Nancy had formed a plan. She would wait for Anne Marie Walters to leave the office and simply follow her. It might prove fruitless to tail the reporter, but then again, something might turn up.

Nancy didn't have to wait long. Within a few minutes Ms. Walters came rushing out of the building. She hopped into a sleek sports car and drove away.

At first Nancy didn't know where the reporter was headed.

She followed the woman's car past Preston Park, over the drawbridge, and along a series of winding roads. It wasn't until she came over the top of a hill that Nancy recognized the area. They were on the road that ran past the entrance to the naval base.

Ahead of her, the reporter's car was pulling up to

the gate. The guard checked his clipboard, then waved her through.

Nancy quickly put on her friendliest smile and drove up to the guard.

"Excuse me," she said, raising her voice to sound like a really excited teenager. "Wasn't that Anne Marie Walters who just drove in?" She fidgeted in her seat as if she could barely control her happiness.

The guard smiled back. "Yes, it was. Do you know Ms. Walters?"

"Not really," Nancy replied. "But I've read everything she's ever written. Is there any chance I could catch up to her to ask for an autograph?"

"I'm afraid not, miss," said the guard.

Nancy looked really disappointed. "But you let *her* onto the base."

"She had an appointment with the head of security," said the guard.

"The head of security," Nancy repeated softly. Then she smiled at the guard. "Well, thanks anyway." She backed away from the gate, waved goodbye, and drove off.

Nancy didn't need to question the guard any further. She knew who was in charge of security at the base. All she wanted to find out now was why Anne Marie Walters had raced off to meet with Commander Adam Daindridge.

7

A Cry in the Mist

So Anne Marie Walters had gone to see Commander Daindridge, Nancy thought. But why? The obvious answer was that Ms. Walters was still working on the Karl Braden case. But Nancy couldn't help but wonder why she had charged out so soon after meeting with her.

She turned the car onto the road that led back into town. Nancy decided to pick Laura up at the restaurant. She wasn't sure what her next move should be, but she hoped the drive would give her a chance to focus her thoughts. She figured Laura would like the ride, too.

Nancy gazed up at the tall pine trees growing on either side of the road. Thin shafts of sunlight cut

59

through their branches, leaving small circles of light on the pine needle floor.

Abruptly, the road opened up onto a street that led to the drawbridge. As Nancy approached, she saw a long line of cars waiting to cross. The bridge was up. The entire center section had risen some sixty feet, like a giant elevator, so that a large ship would have enough room to pass under. Nancy watched as a large freighter slowly made its way under the bridge.

Nancy realized there was nothing to do but wait. She shifted into park and leaned her head back against the seat. Soon she found herself thinking about Ms. Walters again.

Was the reporter simply guessing, or did she really have information that could damage Karl Braden's name?

Nancy wondered if Karl Braden really could have been involved in some crime—smuggling, perhaps? Was that why he had gone out in his boat that evening, in spite of the storm? And if he *was* a smuggler, how would Laura take the news? Nancy didn't want to be the person to have to tell her.

Nancy also wondered if Ms. Walters might only be playing some kind of game with Laura. But why? To get Laura to give her information?

"So many questions," Nancy whispered to herself. "And so little to go on." She gazed out the window at the sunlight sparkling on the water. "I don't even know if there was a real crime committed," she thought out loud. "But someone is definitely trying to convince Laura that her father—or his ghost—has come back." Nancy quickly pushed the idea of a ghost out of her mind. It wasn't possible that Karl Braden had returned from the dead.

A few minutes later, the freighter cleared the bridge. The center section lowered, and traffic quickly began to cross into town.

During the time she had spent waiting on the bridge, Nancy had decided to find out as much as she could about Anne Marie Walters.

Nancy was too late to pick Laura up, so she headed back to the newspaper office. Perhaps Ms. Walters had left something on her desk that would tell Nancy why she had taken off so quickly for a meeting with Daindridge.

Once inside the building, Nancy waited by a pay phone until the receptionist was distracted. Then she moved quickly past the reception desk and down the corridor to the newsroom. The large open area was practically empty. Nancy wondered where everyone was. Then she noticed an office full of people at the far end of the room. The office had a large glass window, and Nancy could see the six or seven *Herald* reporters sitting inside. It appeared that they were in a meeting with the editor in chief. He was doing most of the talking.

The rest of the desk was pretty messy. There were piles of folders, files, and several stacks of typewritten pages. There were also two half-empty coffee containers and a partially eaten toasted corn muffin.

Despite Ms. Walters's neat appearance, Nancy thought, the woman was not very neat.

Nancy quickly searched the desktop. She noticed that most of the papers appeared to be unfinished stories by Ms. Walters. There were also some memos from the editor in chief, urging the reporter to complete her stories as quickly as possible. Some of the memos were several days old.

Nancy continued to search the desk until she came across a folder marked Braden. When she opened it, she found a newspaper photograph of Karl Braden. The photo was part of the story Ms. Walters had written about the sinking of his boat.

Stapled to the photo was a slip of paper with several names and phone numbers scribbled on it. Nancy wasn't very surprised to see Commander Adam Daindridge and Sam Beaumont on it. Penciled in next to Beaumont's name were the words "Worked with Braden. Check out first."

What specifically had Sam Beaumont worked on with Karl Braden? Nancy wondered.

She quickly closed the folder and returned it to its original position on the desk—beneath the corn muffin.

Nancy was about to leave when she spotted the reporter's desk calendar. Nancy hoped that Ms. Walters might have written down something about her appointment with Commander Daindridge.

That day's calendar page, however, did not contain

any mention of the commander or a meeting at the naval base.

That's strange, Nancy thought. Either Ms. Walters suddenly decided to go see him, or she didn't want anyone to know about their meeting.

But there were a few notes jotted on that day's date. "Craven Cove," the reporter had written. And Sam Beaumont's name appeared a few lines farther down the page.

Nancy realized that everything was pointing toward Craven Cove. Karl Braden's boat had gone down just off the cove. Laura had seen the mysterious man in the cave while at the cove. And now, Anne Marie Walters was interested in that same spot.

Nancy decided to go back to Craven Cove as soon as possible.

Feeling that she had learned all she could, Nancy stepped away from the desk and peeked out into the newsroom.

Fortunately, there was no one in sight. As Nancy made her way back across the room, she noticed that the reporters were still in with the editor in chief.

Nancy was almost to the door when it suddenly swung open. There stood the woman who had directed Nancy to Ms. Walters's desk earlier.

"May I help you?" Thomasina asked. She looked at Nancy closely. "Weren't you in here this morning?"

Nancy thought fast. "I came back to see Ms. Walters. I knocked and she doesn't seem to be in."

"Oh, the princess," said Thomasina, her eyes narrowing. "She ran out a while ago. There's no telling when she'll be back."

"That's too bad," said Nancy. She tried to ease past the woman. "Well, I guess I'll drop by another time, then."

"Do you want to leave a message for her?" Thomasina asked.

"No, thank you," Nancy replied. "I'll come back."

"That would be a mistake." The woman shot a dirty look at Ms. Walters's work area.

"You really don't like Ms. Walters, do you?" Nancy asked.

"She's an ambitious woman who'll stop at nothing to get what she wants," Thomasina replied. "This is a small pond—"

"And Ms. Walters wants to be the big fish?" Nancy guessed.

"Oh, she already is." A wicked smile appeared on Thomasina's face. "She's a barracuda. Have a nice day now."

The woman turned away, and Nancy quickly left the newsroom.

As she passed the reception desk, an idea came to her mind.

"Excuse me," she said to the receptionist. "I'd like to look at some back issues of the *Herald*."

"How far back?" the receptionist asked.

"The past six months," Nancy replied.

The receptionist directed Nancy to a room in the

lower level of the building. The sign on the door read Newspaper Archives.

The small, dimly lit room contained only a few tables and chairs. A microfilm projector was set up at each table.

Nancy noticed an attendant sitting at a desk in the corner. Behind him was a storeroom filled with old newspapers and microfilm files.

The attendant was very friendly and helpful. For the next two hours, Nancy read everything she could find about Karl Braden's accident and the investigation. She went back even further to read all she could about Craven Cove and the naval base. She wasn't sure what she was looking for, but she hoped something would turn up.

The church bells were tolling five o'clock when Nancy finally began to head home. The sun was lost in a dark gray sky that promised more rain.

Once again Nancy's head was filled with questions. How was it possible that a town that looked so peaceful could be a mask for some terrible secret? she wondered. A secret that might hurt Nancy's favorite grade-school teacher, and maybe even destroy a girl's love for her father.

Nancy was still lost in thought as she drove back across the bridge to the Braden home.

She parked her car next to Laura's and went inside the house.

"Is that you, Nancy?" Miss Braden called out.

"It sure is," said Nancy. As she walked into the

kitchen, she knew something was wrong. "What's up?"

Bess and George were standing next to Miss Braden. The schoolteacher held a small slip of pink memo paper in her hand. The three of them looked worried.

"Hi, Nancy," said George. "We just got back from a drive, and—"

"We found this note from Laura," Miss Braden interrupted. "It says that she was going to Craven Cove and that she'd be back by four-thirty." Miss Braden looked up at the clock on the wall. "It's after five now."

"George and I suggested that we drive Miss Braden over to the cove to look around," Bess said. Nancy could see that Bess was concerned about their teacher.

"Sounds like a good idea to me," Nancy said quickly. "Come on, let's go."

The drive to the cove was short. Along the way the girls and Miss Braden kept an eye out for Laura, hoping to see her heading home. But there was no sign of her.

"There's her bike," Bess said, jumping out of the car. "She must still be around here."

Laura's bike lay on the ground, just where the grass met the sand.

"Let's look around," Nancy suggested. "George and I will take the cliff side. Bess, you and Miss Braden can walk along the beach."

A thick fog was rolling in from the sea. Nancy and

her friends could barely see the water's edge. The houses, farther down the beach, were only gray shadows.

As they were about to start searching the cove for Laura, Bess called out, "Look at that!"

Nancy, George, and Miss Braden turned to look in the direction Bess was pointing. Out on the water they could just see the out-of-service lighthouse.

"I thought that lighthouse was supposed to be abandoned," said Bess.

"It is," said Miss Braden. "The town closed it down over six years ago."

Bess inched closer to the schoolteacher. "Then what is that?"

A faint yellowish glow, like a dim cat's eye, was winking on and off through the mist. It appeared as if a light were on in the abandoned lighthouse.

"It looks like it's coming from the base of the lighthouse," said George. "Do you think it's some kind of code?"

"It could be," said Nancy, straining to see the light through the mist. "But it's definitely not Morse code. I know that one. We'll have to check the lighthouse out later."

"We will?" Bess asked with a tremor in her voice.

"Don't worry," Nancy said. She knew how much Bess hated to go into spooky places. "I'll go alone if I have to. But right now we'd better look for Laura. Let's scatter and meet back here in fifteen minutes. Okay?"

Nancy and George quickly started to scale the cliff. But when they looked up, they could see only the jagged mounds of rock poking out of the gathering mist and approaching darkness.

"I hope Laura's not up *there*," said Nancy. She tried to spot the ledge on which she and Laura had stood the first day. "It would be hard to climb up or down. I—"

Suddenly a horrible scream ripped through the air. "Help!"

"That sounded like Laura!" George exclaimed.

"Laura!" Nancy shouted. "Is that you?"

Through the swirling mist, Laura's terrified voice echoed back. "Nancy, I can't hold on! Help me, I'm falling!"

"Nancy," said George anxiously, "where *is* she? I can't see a thing. More fog is rolling in!"

"Come on," Nancy shouted over her shoulder. "We've got to climb! Maybe we'll spot her farther up. Hurry!"

Nancy and George began to scramble up the rocks as fast as they could. Somewhere up on that cliff, Laura Braden might be about to fall. The two girls could only hope that they would reach her in time.

8

What the Gessups Knew

Nancy and George continued to make their way quickly over the loose, jagged rocks. It was difficult to spot handholds through the drifting fog, but in a matter of seconds, the two girls had reached the ledge.

"Laura!" Nancy cried out. "Where are you?"

"Over here," she shouted. "Hurry, I can't hold on much longer!"

Nancy and George flattened themselves against the cliff face and sidestepped along the ledge. At the far end, near the cave, they found Laura hanging on the ledge by her fingers. She was desperately trying to hold on. Twenty feet below, the sea was crashing against the rocky shore.

Nancy grabbed Laura's wrists just as the girl's grip was about to give out. George grabbed Nancy around the waist, and together they pulled Laura to safety.

For a moment they sat on the ledge and tried to catch their breath.

"What happened?" Nancy asked finally.

"I climbed up here and decided to explore the cave," Laura replied. "This is where I saw my father the other day. Remember, Nancy?"

Nancy glanced toward the cave, then back at Laura. "We're still not sure what you saw," she said.

"Well, I am," Laura said. "So I came up here to look for him. That's when I noticed a light in the abandoned lighthouse."

"We saw it, too," said Bess. "It was winking on and off like some kind of signal."

Laura became very excited. "That's right. Anyway, I moved forward a little to watch the light blinking. And then I heard a noise behind me."

"What kind of noise?" Nancy asked.

"It was like the sound of pebbles falling," Laura replied. "I turned around quickly, and that was when the section I was standing on started to crumble, and down I went."

"It's a good thing we came looking for you," said George.

"I'll say," Laura said. "A few more seconds and I would have—" She didn't finish her sentence. The thought of what could have happened clearly filled her with dread.

70

Nancy stood up and looked out over the water toward the abandoned lighthouse. The fog was thick now, and the old structure was nothing more than a faint, ghostly shadow. One thing was certain—the light was no longer flashing.

"I'm not sure," said Nancy, "but it's possible someone was sending a signal to someone who was on this cliff. The pebbles could have been sent flying by someone on this ledge or on one up higher."

"You mean someone could have been up here with Laura?" George asked. She helped the younger girl to her feet.

"It's also possible that the signal was being sent to someone on the beach. We saw it down there," Nancy replied. "Maybe the same man you saw up here the other day was up here again," Nancy continued, thinking out loud. Nancy turned to Laura. "And whoever that man is—he could be connected with that lighthouse."

"I'm convinced there was someone up here with me, and I'm equally convinced he couldn't have been my father," Laura declared. "My father would have helped me."

"I'm sure he would have—if he'd known you were in trouble," Nancy said. "Maybe he couldn't see you in the fog."

"But where did this person who was on the cliff with Laura escape to? Where is he now?" George asked.

"He could have gone up to the top or into the cave.

Either way, he's not here now," Nancy answered. "And it's too foggy to follow anyone."

"So what are we going to do next?" asked George.

"Get down from here and tomorrow we'll go out to that lighthouse and look around," Nancy replied, starting to move along the ledge.

A moment later a yellow beacon from the lighthouse run by the Gessups cut a path through the dense mist.

"We'll visit the Gessups, too," Nancy said. "I want to know why the beacon failed the night of the storm."

"Well, it's old," said George. "It's probably failed plenty of other times."

"No, it hasn't," Laura replied. "The beacon had never failed before the accident." She paused. "And it hasn't failed since then, either."

"Do you think that the lighthouse was sabotaged?" George asked.

"I don't know," Nancy said calmly. "It's a possibility that we'll have to check out tomorrow."

Slowly and carefully the girls continued their descent to the beach. Throughout the climb down, Nancy couldn't shake the uneasy feeling that they were being watched.

Late Thursday morning, after dropping Laura off at work, the girls drove down to the docks.

They parked the car near the bridge and walked

along until they reached a small shed with a bright blue and white sign. The sign read U-Float Boat Rental. Peter Littlefield, Manager.

"This is the place Miss Braden told us about," said Bess. "She said Mr. Littlefield would be happy to rent us a boat."

"Then let's make him happy," Nancy teased as they entered the shed.

But even after filling out several forms, showing her operator's license, and paying for the boat, Nancy found Mr. Littlefield anything but happy to rent to her. In fact, he seemed quite nervous.

"You're sure you can handle her?" the manager asked, following the girls out to one of the boats. He was a very short man, with thinning hair and a chubby face.

"Yes, sir," Nancy replied. She smiled as she and George stepped down into the boat. "I've already shown you my license. And I really have driven motorboats before."

"She has," George said cheerfully as she reached up to help Bess into the boat. "And Nancy can handle a boat well in an emergency, too."

The manager frowned. "Emergency? What emergency?"

"There won't be one, Mr. Littlefield, I promise." Nancy untied the boat from the dock. "We're just going to take a look around the harbor to Craven Cove."

73

"Well, all right," said Mr. Littlefield. He dragged out his words just like Sam Beaumont. "But be careful. And have her back in three hours."

"We will," said Bess, waving as Nancy put the boat in gear and steered toward the open water. She stopped waving when she recognized someone standing beside the rental shed. "Look, there's Mr. Beaumont," she said.

George and Nancy looked back and saw Sam Beaumont watching them. His lips were drawn into a hard, straight line, and his steel gray eyes gleamed with an unnatural brightness.

It was only the reflection from the sun, Nancy told herself. She did stop herself from waving at him, though. His expression looked too fierce.

She watched as Sam Beaumont lowered his head and walked away.

"Was it me," asked George, "or did he seem to be glaring at us?"

"It wasn't just you," Bess agreed. "He looked furious, too. The look on his face gave me the shivers."

Nancy turned her full attention to guiding the boat out of the harbor. The naval base commanded the entire shoreline on their right.

"We'll see a different side of the base as we head for the cove," she said.

"Laura said we'd be able to see it from the Gessups' lighthouse," George added. "It sure looks a lot bigger from the water than it did from the shore."

Once they were clear of the other boats, Nancy opened up the throttle and the boat picked up speed. Soon they were heading toward open water and Craven Cove.

Twenty minutes later, Nancy steered the boat up to the Gessups' dock. The girls tied off the boat and made their way up the winding dirt path to the lighthouse.

Nancy had to knock several times before a short, elderly man with a fringe of pure white hair opened the door.

"Well, if this isn't a surprise," he exclaimed. "More company! Please, come right in." The man bowed slightly as he waved the girls into the lighthouse.

"I'm Ben Gessup." The man wiped his pudgy hand on his overalls, then offered it to the girls.

Nancy quickly introduced herself and her friends. "We're visiting June Braden and her niece, Laura," said Nancy. "We came out to ask you a couple of questions, if you don't mind."

"Not at all," Mr. Gessup said. He seemed genuinely pleased to have some visitors. "I'm sorry it took so long to get to the door. Me and the missus were doing some work on the lamp."

"One of your lamps blew out?" Bess asked.

"Not exactly," Mr. Gessup replied, smiling. "Come on up and I'll explain." The lighthouse keeper moved to a stone staircase. The stairs twisted around a wide, concrete column and rose to the enclosed lighthouse tower. The structure was at least five stories high.

"Up?" Bess swallowed hard. "I don't suppose I could wait for you all down here?" she asked.

"Alone," George said.

Bess looked around at the damp walls, which were filled with cracks and holes. "Do you have mice?" she asked Mr. Gessup.

"Yep." Mr. Gessup grinned and nodded his head. "And sometimes we get their big brothers."

"Last one up is a rotten egg," said Bess. She scrambled past Nancy and George and started up the stairs.

The tower room was circular, with glass windows all around. The only thing inside it was the lighthouse lamp.

The lamp had a huge light bulb with a highly polished disk behind it. The disk reflected the light, increasing the bulb's brightness many times. It was encased in a glass cylinder, and the whole lamp sat on top of a revolving platform.

Mrs. Gessup stood beside the glass case. The elderly woman wore a thick sweater and work pants. She was scrubbing the inside of the case with a brush.

"Company?" she asked when she noticed the three girls. "We don't usually have many visitors here."

"Except Neal Richards," Mr. Gessup said. "Neal's the skipper of the supply boat," he added.

After her husband had introduced the girls, Mrs. Gessup started back to her work.

"With all this moisture, the mildew builds up even inside the glass," she explained, scrubbing away at a

76

greenish stain. "You can't let anything dirty the glass or the lens."

"That's right," said Mr. Gessup. He knelt down and reached into a section underneath the lamp. "You have to keep the turntable greased, too. If the lamp doesn't turn properly, about six miles of ocean will go dark."

"Do you clean it very often?" Nancy asked.

"Once a week," Mr. Gessup replied.

Nancy dropped to her knees beside him. "Do you work on the generator, too?"

"I'll say I do." Slowly Mr. Gessup straightened up and looked at Nancy. "You told me you were friends of the Bradens, didn't you?"

"That's right," said Bess. "Miss Braden used to be our teacher in elementary school."

"Then I guess maybe you're asking about the generator because of Laura's father," Mr. Gessup said. He sounded a little sad.

"Yes, we are." Nancy glanced from Mr. to Mrs. Gessup.

Mrs. Gessup put down her brush and folded her hands together. "Karl was a lovely young man."

Bess's eyes widened. "You knew Mr. Braden?"

"We certainly did," Mrs. Gessup replied. "Next to Neal, Karl Braden was the only person who paid us regular visits."

"When was this?" Nancy asked.

Mr. Gessup scratched his stubby white beard. "He came around in his boat about twice a week. He started visiting about two months before he—before his accident," said Mrs. Gessup. "He just stopped by one day and started chatting away."

"Yep," Mr. Gessup continued. "He talked up a storm about lobster traps, tides, the cove, ships—"

"Excuse me," Nancy interrupted. "Karl Braden asked you about the cove? Do you mean Craven Cove?"

"Yes," said Mrs. Gessup. She walked to the window that overlooked Craven Cove. "Karl asked us a lot of questions about that place. And by the time we got through talking with him, he knew everything there was to know about the tides and the currents in that cove."

Mr. Gessup smiled when he saw the puzzled expressions on the girls' faces.

"When you live in a place for twenty-two years," he said, "you get to know it pretty well."

Nancy walked over and stood next to Mrs. Gessup.

Ben Gessup rubbed his legs a bit. "Yep," he said thoughtfully. "In the past few months, a lot of people have been asking about the cove. First Karl—then that newspaper woman—oh, yes, and that other lobsterman, Sam Beaumont."

"Ms. Walters has been here?" George asked.

"Twice now," Mrs. Gessup replied.

Nancy wasn't surprised to hear Sam Beaumont's name. It was possible that he needed the information to help him set traps. But what had Anne Marie Walters wanted?

Mrs. Gessup began to chuckle. "Even the navy has occasionally asked our advice about the cove."

Nancy suddenly glanced toward the base. "Any specific officer?" she asked.

Mr. Gessup frowned. "Why, yes. A Commander Daindridge, I believe."

"When did all these people become so interested in the cove?" Nancy asked.

"Well, Sam came around once before Karl's accident. And then he stopped by again just the other day."

"And that newspaper woman has been around twice in the past week," Mrs. Gessup added.

"Commander Daindridge was here right after the accident, isn't that right, Mother?" Mrs. Gessup nodded and her husband scratched his beard again. "I think Daindridge was in charge of the search party."

"Has anyone asked you about the other lighthouse?" Bess asked.

"Oh, that old thing," said Mrs. Gessup. She wrinkled up her nose at the tower that stood only a half mile away. "That thing is more trouble than it's worth. I don't know why they don't just tear it down."

"Have you noticed any activity over there lately?" asked Nancy.

"Can't say that I have," Mr. Gessup replied. "But if you're thinking of going over there, be very careful."

"Why?" Bess asked nervously.

"Because it's hazardous," said Mrs. Gessup. "No

79

one has been taking care of it. I'm sure the floor is rotting. It's ready to tumble down."

"Actually, we *were* thinking of going over there," Nancy told the elderly couple. "Just to look around. But I promise we'll be careful."

"There's a keeper's cottage on the other side of the lighthouse," Mr. Gessup said. "Just like ours."

"The side that faces the cove?" asked Nancy.

"Yep," said Mr. Gessup.

Nancy smiled. "Well, we'd better be going," she said. "Thank you so much for talking with us."

The girls started toward the stairwell, but Mr. Gessup stopped them.

"Just so you know," he said, "Donna and me keep this place in tip-top shape. I don't rightly know how those generators could have blown—storm or no storm." Mr. Gessup lowered his head as his wife put her hand on his shoulder. "But tell Karl's daughter I'm real sorry about what happened. I really am."

"We will," Nancy assured him, and the girls began to descend the stairs.

Fifteen minutes later, they were tying off their boat at the dock of the other lighthouse.

The Gessups had been right. It was obvious that no one was taking care of the area. The docks were rotting and covered with algae.

They made their way toward the lighthouse. Bess still looked squeamish from touching the wet, slimy wood.

All around the building were signs of decay: debris, weeds, and old equipment rusting on the ground.

"That's strange," said Nancy as she tried the door to the lighthouse. "There's no padlock, and the door is unlocked."

Bess glanced around nervously. "And we're going in, right?"

"I promise we won't stay long," said Nancy, trying to calm her friend.

"Any amount of time is too long when you're going into a spooky-looking place like this." Bess inched closer to her friends.

Nancy carefully pushed on the door, and it slowly opened inward. Despite rust on the hinges, they didn't creak.

Nancy gave them a close inspection. "These hinges have been oiled recently," she said. "That's odd."

The girls walked slowly through the door and into the base of the old building.

"This is scary," said Bess as they stopped in the center of the entryway. The only light came from the open door through which they had just entered.

The inside of the lighthouse looked very much like the one the Gessups took care of, but it was in terrible shape. The walls were covered with mildew and water had seeped in from somewhere, creating small pools all over the floor. The steps were covered with algae and a section of them seemed to have collapsed inward.

81

"Those don't look safe enough for us to climb," said George.

"I agree," Nancy replied. "And we really don't have to go up to the top, anyway. The light we saw came from ground level. Let's try over there," she said, pointing to an old wooden door. "That should connect with the lightkeeper's cottage."

Nancy moved across the floor to the other door. She turned the cold, rusty knob, and the door opened easily.

"Very strange," she whispered.

She was on the ground floor of the cottage. There were three steps that led down to what looked like a living room. The entire place was covered in dirt and grime.

On the girls' left were four windows. All of them had iron bars running vertically from top to bottom.

Straight ahead of them was a table, two wooden chairs, and what looked like canvas lying on the floor.

As she moved farther into the room, Nancy saw a flagstone chimney to her right. The fireplace was black with soot.

She went over to the table and chairs and ran her finger across the surface of the table.

"It's clean," she said, frowning.

"You mean someone might be living here?" Bess asked. She was standing beside another doorway. "This leads to a kitchen, and it looks filthy in there." Bess shuddered at the thought of going into the darkened room.

"Well, this fireplace has certainly been used." George held up a small, burned log. "It looks like someone needed to warm this place up."

"And you'd only need to do that if you were staying here." Nancy moved to a window that faced the cove.

"This window has been wiped clean," said Nancy. "Someone wanted to be able to see clearly."

Nancy was about to check out the fireplace when she noticed something on the floor. She knelt down and picked up a grimy length of rope.

"These are the same types of knots I saw in Laura's rope necklace," said Nancy, holding it up to show the others. "I think it's pretty obvious that someone has been here. But how long ago and for what?"

Nancy looked around the rest of the cottage and found a bedroom. She couldn't tell if it had been used recently.

A few minutes later she, Bess, and George were back in the motorboat, skimming across the calm water to return to the harbor.

The sun was bright in the afternoon sky, and Nancy's mind was racing.

"Anne Marie Walters is definitely out to get something on Karl Braden," she said out loud. "She has a file on him that includes notes about Sam Beaumont and Commander Daindridge."

"Do you think she and the commander could be working together?" asked Bess.

"On what, though?" Nancy asked.

"Maybe Ms. Walters is involved in something illegal, but I don't see how Daindridge fits in." George ran her fingers through her short dark hair and decided not to think about it right then. She just sat back and enjoyed the soft sea spray on her face.

"Me, either," Nancy agreed. "The only thing that's clear is that there's a mystery involving Craven Cove. And everybody we've mentioned may be involved somehow."

"I have an idea," said Bess. "Maybe it's—"

Bess suddenly screamed. The boat rocked back and forth violently after a small explosion sounded in the engine. Clouds of black smoke rushed out from under the floor and dashboard.

The acrid fumes stung the girls' eyes. They could see nothing. Nancy reached down to shut off the engine and yanked back her hand from the terrible heat of the metal key.

All three girls skittered backward, away from the dashboard. Flames shot out from the dashboard, melting paint and singeing wood.

"Nancy, the boat's on fire!" Bess shouted.

9

Sabotage!

"Should we jump overboard?" Bess asked, on the verge of hysteria.

"No. Not if we don't have to," said Nancy. "That water is ice-cold, and the current is very strong."

Suddenly George's eyes widened. "Nancy, look!" she shouted, pointing straight ahead of them.

Their boat was veering toward a pile of rocks that were jutting out of the water.

Nancy knew that they and their boat would be destroyed if they continued their present course.

Desperately, she tried to regain control of the wheel, but it was too hot to handle and flames were spreading across the panel.

George looked down, and under the gunwale she

spotted a fire extinguisher strapped in place. She grabbed it and immediately began spraying the area around the steering wheel.

Nancy took hold of the wheel and turned the boat away from the rocks. "I can't slow down," she cried. "The gears are gone!" Flames were licking around the ignition area, so Nancy couldn't turn the key off.

"Nancy, look out!" Bess screamed. A fire had suddenly sprung up at Nancy's feet.

George aimed the fire extinguisher, and the flames were doused. Nancy turned back to the controls.

"Get rid of the fire around the ignition and engine," she shouted. "We can't risk an explosion. We'll all be blown up." The motor sounded as if it were trying to tear the boat apart now.

"I'm going to radio for help before the wires melt," Nancy told Bess, grabbing the microphone for the two-way radio. "Someone may get here in time, but you two had better prepare to abandon ship!"

Bess lifted a lid beneath her seat and reached into the compartment in which the life jackets were stored. She handed jackets to Nancy and George, then put on her own.

"Mayday! Mayday!" Nancy shouted into the microphone. "This is an emergency! Our boat is on fire a couple of miles off Craven Cove! Mayday, Mayday!"

Nancy repeated the distress call several times before she received an answer from the Coast Guard.

The officer assured her they were on their way at top speed.

By now George had completely extinguished the flames coming up through the floorboards as well as the fire on the control panel. "I think that's about it," she said wearily.

Nancy could touch the key now and cut the engine. The boat slowed to a stop.

"I'd better check the motor," said George. She tried to open a hatch in the deck of the boat, but the brass handle was too hot.

"Let me help." Bess found an old cloth, and together she and George pulled the door open.

Black smoke came billowing out of the chamber. The boat's engine and wiring below were a charred, smoky mess, but there appeared to be no sign of flames.

To be safe, George sprayed the entire area until the extinguisher ran out of foam. The fire was definitely out.

With tremendous sighs of relief, the girls moved to the rear of the boat and sat down, exhausted.

"I think Mr. Littlefield is going to be slightly upset," Bess said.

"Maybe just a bit," said Nancy, returning her friend's smile. "But he's not going to be half as upset as I am right now. That fire was very suspicious."

"It could have been the wiring. Or maybe some oil rag left too near the engine."

"That doesn't explain the small explosion we heard just before the flames started," Nancy replied. She leaned forward and looked down into the engine compartment. "I can't wait to have somebody check this out."

A few minutes later a Coast Guard cutter came rushing up beside their boat. The crew helped the girls board the cutter, then checked out the charred boat. After a few minutes they took the damaged vessel in tow and headed back to port.

"I knew I shouldn't have rented a boat to you," said an angry Mr. Littlefield. The manager was staring at the damaged boat as Nancy and a Coast Guard lieutenant inspected the engine.

"But it wasn't our fault," George insisted. "There was a loud bang, and the next thing we knew, smoke and flames were everywhere."

"It's true," said Bess. "We almost had to jump into the ocean."

"Well, I check all my boats at the start of each day," said Mr. Littlefield. "And that boat was in fine shape this morning."

"Maybe it was," Nancy said. She and the Coast Guard officer had just climbed onto the dock. "But something went terribly wrong with your engine."

"That's right," said the lieutenant. "There is evidence that a small explosion did damage the gears and the engine. If the girls hadn't acted as quickly as they did, that boat would have crashed or sunk."

"But I—I don't understand," Mr. Littlefield stammered.

The officer made a few notes on his clipboard and

handed Mr. Littlefield a card. "We'll have to investigate this further, sir. Please have your insurance company call me."

"Honest," Mr. Littlefield said, "I didn't know there was anything wrong with that boat." The rental manager sounded very upset.

"We believe you," Nancy said calmly. "And I'm sure it will all work out."

As Mr. Littlefield walked over to inspect the damage, Nancy turned to Bess and George.

"I'm also pretty sure that this was no accident," she said. "Even the Coast Guard officer said that the fire looked very suspicious."

"You mean someone might have deliberately sabotaged our boat?" George asked.

"It's possible," Nancy replied.

"But who?" Bess looked around. "And when would they have had the chance?"

"There were only two opportunities that I can think of," Nancy replied. "While we were visiting the Gessups, or while we were exploring the abandoned lighthouse."

"What about while we were renting the boat?" Bess asked. "Remember, we saw Mr. Beaumont hanging around the dock? And he didn't look very friendly."

"That's possible," said Nancy. She started walking toward their parked car. "But it'll take time to find out for certain. Meanwhile, we'd better pick up Laura from work. If we're in danger, so is she!"

* * *

89

On the way to the restaurant, Nancy tried to put the pieces together. But all she came up with were more questions all centered around Craven Cove and Karl Braden.

Laura was in a great mood when the girls arrived. "I'm almost finished," she said cheerfully, leading the girls to a table by a window. "You sit here and order anything you want. My treat."

George's brown eyes twinkled. "That's a dangerous thing to say to Bess at a restaurant."

"Thanks a lot," Bess said with a smile.

"Don't mind them," said Nancy. "They do this all the time. But I'm really glad to see you so happy, Laura."

"Well, you're part of the reason," Laura said. "Now that you're investigating my father's accident, I just know we'll find him—and everything will be fine."

Nancy cast a quick glance at Bess and George. "There are still a lot of questions to be answered," she said.

Laura leaned in closer to the girls, her eyes sparkling with excitement. "I know that, Nancy. But at least now I'm sure he's alive. If he's hurt, you'll find him. And if he's in trouble, I'm sure you can help him."

Nancy shifted uncomfortably in her seat. Laura was putting all her hopes on Nancy to solve an extremely difficult puzzle and find a man who was probably dead.

Nancy wasn't at all sure that Karl Braden was alive.

90

But if he was, she had an uncomfortable feeling that the solution to the case might put Laura's father in jail. Why else would he have gone into hiding for six months? He must have something to hide.

"At least I can look people in the eye now and tell them they were wrong," Laura continued.

"What do you mean?" George asked.

"Well, Commander Daindridge was in here for lunch. I told him we had definite proof that my father was alive," Laura replied.

"What exactly did you say?" Nancy asked.

Laura straightened up. "I told him about the man at the cove and the knotted cord. Why?"

"I didn't want anyone to know what we'd discovered yet," Nancy replied. "Not until we knew a little more, at least."

"Well, I had to tell Commander Daindridge," said Laura. "He and my dad were such good friends. And he thought Daddy was dead like everybody else did."

Nancy gave Laura a big smile and opened her menu. "Well, no harm done, I guess," she said. "And I think I'll take you up on that late lunch offer. How about a chef's salad and a diet ginger ale?"

"That sounds good to me," said George.

Bess studied the menu carefully. "I'll have the seafood platter with french fries and plenty of tartar sauce."

"What happened to your diet?" Nancy asked.

"We still have three more days left of our vacation," Bess said. "I'll work it off."

91

"I'll put your orders in," said Laura. "Then I'll try to finish up quickly and join you."

After Laura had gone into the kitchen, Nancy sighed heavily.

"I wish Laura hadn't said anything to Commander Daindridge," she said. "If her father *is* hiding from the law, it will put the commander in a bad position."

"We're not in a great position, either," said Bess. "Don't forget, it seems as if someone tried to drown us in the ocean."

"And I'd like to know why," said George. She ran her fingers through her hair. "It couldn't have been anyone trying to stop us from visiting the lighthouses. Nothing happened until we were on our way back."

"Maybe the saboteur didn't time things right," said Nancy. She sat back and folded her arms. "Let's look at what we know so far. It might help."

Bess began counting off on her fingers. "First, we know that Karl Braden's boat went down in a storm six months ago."

"And Ms. Walters's story said that only a small amount of the wreckage was found," Nancy added. "Something about that bothers me."

"A good-sized wave can totally destroy a boat," George said. "My father once told me—"

"I feel like something's missing," Nancy said.

"Well, I'll keep talking while you think," said Bess. She continued counting on her fingers. "We know Laura believes that her father is alive. *And* that someone who resembles him was sneaking around Craven Cove two days ago. Unless she imagined it."

"And speaking of the cove," George broke in, "someone in the abandoned lighthouse was signaling to the cove or cliffs, remember?"

"And let's not forget the late night delivery of Laura's knotted necklace," said Bess. "The same one that her father gave her years earlier."

"Someone could have broken into the Bradens' house and stolen the necklace," said George.

"Then they might have come back that night and placed it in her window," Bess added.

"And this person wore special shoes," Nancy said softly. She was still deep in thought. "Shoes worn by fishermen and lobstermen."

"Laura thinks that her father was the late-night caller," said Bess. "And I hope that's who it was— and not a you-know-what."

"I don't believe we're dealing with any ghost in this case," Nancy said. "There are too many things that point to a human being. The sabotage of our boat, for instance, and the man Laura saw in the cave."

"Good." Bess sighed. "That means the human suspects are Ms. Walters—"

"A rude and nosy reporter," George grumbled.

"Commander Daindridge," Bess continued.

"Head of the navy base security and friend of Karl Braden," said George.

"And Sam Beaumont," Bess put in.

"A lobsterman who probably wears that kind of shoe." George seemed pleased with her deduction. "And he was at the dock when we left to go to the lighthouse, right?"

"But he's also an old friend of Laura's father," Bess pointed out. "Would he do anything to scare her?"

"Not likely," George said, sounding disappointed.

Nancy placed her head in her hands. "This would be so much easier if we knew what crime had been committed, if any. Without that one piece of information, we could go on guessing like this forever."

"Take it easy, Nancy," said Bess. "Don't blow your top."

Slowly Nancy's face lit up. "Blow my top," she repeated. "That's it!"

The two cousins stared at their friend.

"That's what I couldn't remember," Nancy went on. "The day we met Sam Beaumont, he said to me, 'Karl's engine blew and he went down.'"

"So?" said Bess and George together. They sounded confused.

"Not one report, not one newspaper story, *no one* said anything about an explosion!"

"Oh, Nancy," said George. She put her hand to her lips. "Do you mean what I think you do?"

"What do you think she means?" Bess looked first at Nancy, then at George. "What *do* you mean, Nancy?"

"There may have been an explosion on Karl

Braden's boat before it sank," Nancy said slowly. "And there was an explosion on our boat, too—"

Bess's face paled. "Which almost went down, just as his did."

"Exactly," George agreed.

"That means that Laura's father may have been murdered," Nancy said.

"But if he's not dead . . ." Bess's voice trailed away.

"Then it was only *attempted* murder," Nancy said. "Either way, there's a very dangerous person out there who'll do anything to find Karl Braden if he isn't dead and will stop anyone else from finding him."

"Including Laura or us," said Bess.

Another waitress delivered their lunch order.

Bess stared down at the platter filled with shrimps, scallops, and haddock.

"Is this conversation causing you to lose your appetite?" George teased.

"Are you kidding?" Bess said. She unfolded her napkin and picked up her fork. "I'm just waiting for the tartar sauce."

The girls were in better spirits when they left the restaurant. Laura had to stay for a few minutes to talk to the manager, so Nancy, Bess, and George offered to get the car.

They were four cars away from their own in the parking lot when Nancy noticed that their car hood was up. She could just see the back of a man working under the hood.

"Do you think he's planting a bomb?" whispered Bess.

"I don't know," Nancy replied. "But I intend to find out."

The girls quietly ran toward the car. They were within a few feet of the vehicle when the man stood up suddenly, slammed the hood down, and turned around.

Nancy found herself face-to-face with Sam Beaumont!

10

Beaumont's Warning

"What were you doing under our hood?" Nancy asked the lobsterman.

At first Sam Beaumont looked startled, but as Nancy and her friends drew closer, he grew more and more annoyed.

"I was just checking your motor," he said. There was anger in his voice, as if he felt the girls had no right to be in the parking lot.

"Checking it for what?" George asked.

"For things that could go wrong," the lobsterman replied evenly. His dark eyes narrowed as he met each girl's gaze. "Especially when people snoop."

"What cxactly do you mcan?" asked Nancy.

"I warned you from the beginning," Sam replied.

"Leave things be, I said. They'll work themselves out in the end. But you wouldn't listen."

"We haven't done anything, except try to help Laura and her aunt," George said. "What's wrong with that?"

Sam Beaumont took a step toward her. "Maybe you haven't realized it yet, but you three nearly lost your lives today."

"And you're saying it wasn't an accident?" Nancy's remark was more a statement than a question.

"I'm saying—" The lobsterman suddenly stopped speaking, looking as if he felt he had said too much already.

"What are you saying, Mr. Beaumont?" Nancy demanded. "And what did you mean when you told me that Karl Braden's engine *blew?*"

Sam Beaumont ignored Nancy's questions and started to walk away. But after a few feet he stopped and turned back. "Watch yourself, Nancy Drew. There are dangerous forces at work here. Forces you know nothing about—and can't possibly beat." Then he continued walking.

"What did he mean by 'dangerous forces'?" Bess asked. "I thought there weren't any ghosts in this case."

"I don't know what he meant," said Nancy. Carefully she raised the hood of the car and began systematically to examine the engine.

"Did he plant something?" George asked. She and Bess peered over Nancy's shoulder.

"It doesn't look like it," Nancy replied, frowning.

"Excuse me," came a voice from behind the hood. "Are you girls having engine trouble?"

The three stood up and saw Anne Marie Walters leaning against their car. The reporter looked extremely smug.

"We're just checking," said Nancy. She didn't want to tell Ms. Walters anything about her suspicions. "We thought we heard a strange noise."

The reporter smiled her crooked smile. "Oh? Do you mean—like an explosion?"

The girls exchanged surprised looks.

"Don't be so stunned, ladies," said Ms. Walters. "The whole town is talking about your near-fatal accident. I understand the Coast Guard is looking into the matter."

"Our motor caught fire," Nancy replied cautiously. "And no one is sure how it happened—yet."

Ms. Walters walked around to the front of the car and glanced at the engine. "It was probably something simple," she said. "But it certainly does give one reason to wonder."

"And exactly what *does* one wonder?" asked Bess, mimicking the reporter.

"Whether it was an accident, for starters," Ms. Walters replied. "And if not, then why would anyone try to hurt a visiting teenage detective? Especially when she isn't investigating anything." The reporter raised her eyebrows. "Or is she?"

99

"I'm simply trying to help a friend," Nancy said calmly.

"A friend whose late—excuse me, I mean *missing* —father has recently been seen in the area?"

Nancy's mouth dropped open.

The reporter glanced at the car motor one more time, then began strolling away. "Things are getting very hot for you around here, Ms. Drew," she called back. "Cooperate with me, before it's too late. *Ciao!*"

Ms. Walters's car was parked a few feet away. She slipped in behind the wheel and drove off.

"That woman is the pushiest person I have ever met," said George.

"Most reporters have to be," Bess explained. "It comes with the press card."

"I'm not so sure Anne Marie Walters is after only a story," Nancy said. "She said I'd better cooperate with her before it's too late. That could have been a warning."

"And if it was?" asked George.

Nancy watched the reporter's car disappear down the street. "Then she's involved in whatever is going on around here."

"Let's follow her," Bess suggested.

"Not until I've finished looking over this car," Nancy said. She moved around to the other side and checked the radiator. "We still don't know what Sam Beaumont was up to."

Nancy spent another five minutes searching the car.

She had just closed the hood when Laura came running up to join them.

She was out of breath and seemed very upset.

"What's wrong?" Nancy asked in alarm.

"I was leaving the restaurant when that awful reporter drove up." Laura leaned against the car and inhaled deeply. "She caught me at the front door and said some horrible things."

"She's just trying to stir up dirt about your father," George said. "But don't worry—"

"That's not what she wanted to speak to me about," Laura said with a frown. "She told me you were almost killed today. And she says my father is responsible!"

11

A Trail to the Sea

Laura Braden dropped her canvas bag onto the ground. "Nancy, what's going on? Why is my father hiding? And why is someone trying to hurt us because we're looking for him?"

"I'm not sure," Nancy replied, brushing a lock of hair from her eyes. "All I know so far is that your father was very curious about Craven Cove."

"That's right," said George. "He asked the Gessups all about it."

"My father took me there all the time. He told me all kinds of stories about the place. You know, the soldiers, the fort, the smuggling."

"I remember your telling me that," said Nancy. "But Craven Cove keeps coming up in this case. Your father's boat went down there. We were at the cove when you thought you saw that man. And those signal flashes were directed at the cove."

Laura looked confused. "But what could be going on there that would cause someone to try to hurt you?"

"The same thing that your father may have discovered," said Nancy. And possibly have been involved with, Nancy thought to herself.

"What do you mean?" Laura asked.

"I'm not positive," Nancy said, "but I believe his boat may have been sabotaged like ours."

Laura looked both angry and frightened as Nancy explained about the explosion on their boat. But Nancy made a point of not mentioning her suspicions about Sam Beaumont.

"So you suspect that someone planted an explosive on his boat?" Laura asked.

"Yes, I do," Nancy said. "But I don't know who or why—yet."

"Nancy." Laura's voice trembled, and a single tear ran down her cheek. "Do you think my father is in real danger now?"

"I don't know," Nancy answered softly. "But *if* he is alive and in hiding, I think he'll be safe."

"Safe from whom?" asked Laura, wiping her eyes with her hands.

"I don't know. But I promise we'll find out—and soon." Nancy gave Laura's shoulder a gentle squeeze. "Come on, let's go home."

Bess handed Laura a tissue from her pocket.

"Yeah," she said, trying to sound cheerful, "maybe your aunt has something yummy for dinner."

"You just ate lunch," George said, shaking her head.

"I know," Bess replied. "I'm just planning ahead."

Laura gave the other girls a faint smile, picked up her bag, and climbed into the car.

As Bess scrambled in next to Laura, George turned to Nancy. "Can't we go to the police with any of this?"

"Not yet," said Nancy. "We don't know the whole story. Besides, the police, the Coast Guard, and the navy all believe that Karl Braden is dead. I don't think we can convince them otherwise without more proof. And—" Nancy hesitated, then glanced over her shoulder. Laura and Bess were deep in conversation.

"And?" George asked. She dropped her voice to a whisper. "You mean we still don't know if Laura's father is alive, right? And if he's guilty of anything."

Nancy nodded.

"Do you still think this case might involve smuggling?" George asked.

"It seems logical," Nancy replied. "Smuggling is common in the area. Smugglers always operate near the ocean. This is a perfect harbor. Yes, I think the case has to involve smuggling."

By the time the girls reached the Braden house, Laura was drained.

Nancy talked her into lying down for a while, and

Bess agreed to keep an eye on her. Miss Braden hadn't arrived home yet.

"Since I've been elected to watch over Laura, I guess you two are going somewhere," Bess said.

"We are," Nancy replied. "I want to check out the woods in back of the house while there's still some daylight."

"What are you looking for?" Bess asked.

"That's where our visitor disappeared the other night," Nancy said. "I didn't see anything yesterday, but I want to try again. We'll only be gone a little while. Maybe George will see more than I did."

Bess smiled. "Don't worry about me. There are some delicious homemade cookies in the kitchen, and a great dance movie on TV. I'll be very happy."

A few minutes later Nancy and George left the house and entered the woods.

"Which way?" asked George.

"Down here." Nancy pointed to a narrow trail. "These woods would be too thick to go tearing through in the dark, so I figure our suspect took the easiest route. Let's see if I'm right."

It was very slow going at first. The woods were thick and damp. Many broken branches crisscrossed the trail, making it difficult to push through.

Finally the woods opened out onto a lush, green clearing.

There was a road to the right, and the girls could see several large houses in the distance. Ahead of them lay a small inlet, leading out to the river.

"I think Craven Cove is across the harbor to the left," said Nancy as they approached the shoreline.

George looked excited. "Someone could have brought a boat in here," she said, "and then sneaked up to the Bradens' house and left the necklace."

George was about to take a step forward when Nancy stopped her.

"I think our mystery caller did just that." Nancy knelt down on the dry, sunbaked mud. "Because here is a footprint with the same grooved pattern."

George knelt down beside her. "It's pointing toward the water. Too bad the tide washed away the rest of the prints."

"Don't worry," said Nancy. "At least this proves that our visitor came by boat. And a boat suggests a fisherman."

"Or a lobsterman," George added.

Before Nancy could respond, the girls heard the sharp sound of a branch cracking behind them.

They whirled around to find Commander Daindridge standing a few feet away.

"Or a sailor," Nancy whispered.

"This is a lousy place to look for seashells," the commander said, amused.

Nancy and George returned his smile. "Hi, Commander," they called out.

As the girls stood up, Nancy deliberately stepped on the footprint. She already knew the pattern and there was another sample in the Bradens' backyard. But right now, she didn't want anyone else to see it.

The commander strolled over to the girls. "May I suggest the beach in the next town up the coast? It's not far from here."

"We were just out walking around," said George. "There's still so much of this area that we haven't seen yet."

"Yes, it is beautiful around here," said the commander. He took in a deep breath and let it out slowly.

"I'm surprised to meet you here," said Nancy.

"You shouldn't be," Commander Daindridge replied. "I was driving along the road when I spotted you two. I live in the third house on the left."

Nancy spotted the two-story Colonial in the distance. "Does your house face the water?" she asked.

"Yes, it does." The commander headed down to the shoreline. "And I have a small dock with a sleek little powerboat. I cruise this area every chance I get." The commander turned to Nancy. "As a matter of fact, Karl and I used to go fishing along here."

"Did Mr. Beaumont ever go with you?" Nancy asked.

"Sam?" The commander smiled and adjusted his hat. "It's difficult to get Sam away from his lobsters. He's always kept to himself."

Nancy seemed puzzled. "I thought Laura's father and he were old friends."

"They were," Commander Daindridge replied. "But after what happened—well, their friendship cooled off a bit."

"What happened?" George asked eagerly.

"Karl married Sam's high-school sweetheart," said Commander Daindridge with a shrug. "I thought everybody knew that."

"No one told us," Nancy said. She thought Miss Braden had said that Karl and his wife were high-school sweethearts. Why was Daindridge lying?

"Well, Sam was pretty upset about it," said the commander. "He has a pretty hot temper. Once I even thought he and Karl were going to come to blows about it, but they never did. Then, after Laura was born, things changed."

Nancy thrust her hands into her jacket pockets and looked out over the water. She was trying to decide how much she should tell the commander about what they knew when he said suddenly, "Laura told me that you think Karl is alive."

Nancy said nothing—she didn't know why he had just lied to her.

"If it's true," the commander continued, "then you should tell me where he's hiding."

"We don't know where he is," said Nancy. "We're not even sure if he's alive. Sam Beaumont said we should leave things be."

"In fact," George said, "he insisted that we do just that."

The officer laughed out loud. "Don't let Sam put a scare into you. As I said, he's a very private man with a hot temper. He likes people to mind their own business, that's all."

Nancy wondered what Sam Beaumont would do if someone didn't.

"Well," the commander said, "I better be getting home." He started walking up the slope to the road. "See you around," he called back.

Nancy and George watched the commander get into his car and drive away.

"Well, we sure learned something there," George said enthusiastically. "Now we know that Sam Beaumont has a temper. He was jealous of Karl Braden, too. Maybe he wasn't the friend Laura thought he was. What do you think, Nancy?"

Nancy didn't answer. She was too busy watching the commander's car ease down the road. "That's funny," she muttered.

"What is?" asked George.

"Commander Daindridge is the only person who didn't mention our boating accident," Nancy replied. "Everyone else seems to have heard about it."

"Maybe he didn't hear about it because he was on the base," George offered.

"Maybe," Nancy said, but she wasn't convinced. "You know, the other place that this case seems to center around is the naval base."

"So what does that mean?"

"I don't know, George," said Nancy slowly. "I really don't know."

That evening the moon was bright and full, with only thin streams of clouds drifting across its face.

Nancy, Bess, and George looked up at the sky as they stood outside after dinner at Captain Dan's. They were waiting for Laura and Miss Braden to follow them out.

"It's too bad we have only three more days in Dover," said Bess.

"It sure is," George agreed. "This is such a romantic place." She turned to Nancy. "I bet you wish Ned was here." Ned Nickerson was Nancy's longtime boyfriend.

"That would be nice," Nancy said. She smiled at the thought. "But with all that's happened lately, I don't think we'd have had much time together."

Just then, Miss Braden and her niece came out of the restaurant.

"I hope you girls enjoyed your dinner," Miss Braden said cheerfully.

"Everything was wonderful," Bess assured her. "I couldn't eat another mouthful."

Miss Braden caught up to Nancy and Laura, who were walking ahead. "Nancy," the teacher began. Her face looked sad.

"Yes, Miss Braden?" Nancy asked.

"If my brother *is* alive," she said, "what do you suppose he is hiding from? And why is he putting my niece—and my friends—in so much danger?"

Nancy slowed down so Bess and George could catch up. "I think the answer involves Craven Cove, and one of three suspects."

"Who?" asked Laura.

"You're not going to like this," Nancy said hesitantly.

Miss Braden's face grew stern. "Tell us anyway. We need to get to the bottom of all this."

"I suspect either Ms. Walters, Commander Daindridge, or Sam Beaumont is involved," Nancy said. "And smuggling may be the motive."

"Couldn't you be wrong about that?" Miss Braden asked.

"I could," Nancy replied, "but I don't think so. And I'd like you to help me find out which person it is."

"How?" Laura asked.

"By inviting Commander Daindridge and Mr. Beaumont to lunch tomorrow," Nancy said. "If I can get them talking in the same room, maybe they'll reveal something that will point to a solution. We can worry about Ms. Walters later."

Miss Braden and Laura were silent as they walked into the parking lot. Nancy realized that neither of them really wanted to believe that a close friend was responsible for what was happening to them.

But by the time they reached Laura's car, the teacher and her niece had come to a decision.

"All right," said Miss Braden. "I don't like being dishonest, but if you really think it will help—"

"It will, Miss Braden," Nancy assured her. "Now all we have to do is—" Suddenly she froze, staring straight ahead.

The others followed Nancy's gaze to Laura's car.

There, on the windshield, someone had drawn some kind of a creature in white paint.

"What is that?" Bess asked nervously.

"It looks like a bird," said George. "Vandals must have done it."

The girls all looked at Laura as she let out a little gasp. Her face was white and her mouth hung slack. Finally she found her voice. "It's not just any bird," she said. "It's an albatross—the ancient sea symbol of doom!"

12

Braden's Secret

"Yes, it's definitely an albatross," Nancy said, and put an arm around Laura to calm her.

"We must call the police right away," Miss Braden insisted. "The person who left this may be the same one who tampered with your boat."

"Maybe," said Nancy, "but I don't think we should call the police just yet. Someone thinks we're getting too close and wants to scare us off. As long as the person is still giving warnings, I believe we'll be safe. If the police get involved, the culprit will simply stay low until this blows over. We'll never find out what happened to Laura's father, or who's behind all this."

Miss Braden looked doubtful. "I don't know what to say, Nancy. I would never forgive myself if anything happened to you."

"We'll be extra careful," Nancy promised. "Please give me a little more time. For Laura's sake and for your brother's."

"All right," said Miss Braden, throwing up her hands. "You always were a headstrong girl. I'll give you one more day. But any more threats and—"

"I promise we'll be very careful," Nancy said quickly. "And if things get too rough, we'll call in the police."

"Very well," Miss Braden said. "Now, how about someone getting some paper towels so we can clean this awful drawing off?"

"Yes ma'am," Bess said cheerfully. She and George hurried back into the restaurant.

"And tomorrow," Miss Braden went on, "we'll have your little gathering of suspects. But I do hope none of our friends is a crook."

It took only a few minutes for the girls to clean the paint off the windshield. Then Laura drove them all home.

By the time they entered the house, everyone was in better spirits.

"So who wants to play a game or watch TV?" Bess asked as they entered the kitchen.

"Count me out," Nancy replied. She turned to Laura. "I'd like to go through your father's papers again. I may have overlooked a clue in there somewhere."

"I'll help you," Laura said.

"We'll all help," Miss Braden insisted. "I'll do anything to help clear up this case."

Laura headed for the staircase. "Then let's start snooping. Attic, here we come."

The floors and ceiling of the Bradens' attic were bare wood. Every inch of the room was stuffed with old trunks, furniture, paintings, clothes, and newspapers.

Everyone crowded into the corner in which Miss Braden kept her brother's personal things.

"Here they are," said the teacher as she emptied two boxes. "Let's see. Records, business papers, photos, code book, letters—"

"Just a minute," said Nancy. "May I see the code book?"

"Certainly," said Miss Braden. She handed the volume to Nancy.

Karl Braden's code book was very old. The outside was dusty and worn, and the copyright date was over twenty-five years old. Nancy examined the book carefully.

"What are you looking for?" George asked.

"I'm not sure," Nancy replied, "but Laura said her father handled coded messages as a radio engineer at the naval base. The other day we saw coded flashes coming from the abandoned lighthouse. I was just wondering if—" Suddenly she stopped. "The back cover feels funny," she said.

"What do you mean?" Miss Braden asked.

Nancy began peeling the inside paper off the back cover. "It's a lot thicker than the front cover. The glue is different from the rest of the book, too. It's rubbery."

Nancy peeled the paper back, and a folded sheet of paper fell to the floor. She quickly picked it up and opened it.

The page was filled with columns of numbers and letters, all jumbled together.

"It's a code!" Nancy exclaimed.

"Can you read it?" asked Bess.

"No," Nancy said. "I've never seen this type of code before. This could be a message, or even the key to the code itself."

"It's probably one of Karl's old codes from childhood," Miss Braden said.

"I don't think so," Nancy replied. "This feels like computer paper. There are little perforations along the sides, and computers were not very common back then. Also, the paper is not brittle and yellow."

Nancy handed the page to Miss Braden. "Is this your brother's handwriting?"

"It looks like it," Miss Braden replied, examining the paper. "His penmanship was always terrible."

Laura peeked over her aunt's shoulder. "What does it mean?"

"Your father must have been working on this code," Nancy explained, feeling charged with excitement. "For some reason, he didn't want anybody to see it, so

116

he hid it here, away from his family, friends, and co-workers."

George took the paper. "Can you tell how long it's been in the book?"

"I'd guess several months at the most," Nancy replied. "There are no signs of age."

"So he could have hidden this just before the accident," Bess said.

"He could have," said Nancy.

"How can we find out what it means?" asked George.

"The only way is to hope Karl Braden is still alive and find him," Nancy answered.

Miss Braden gave Nancy an admiring glance. "You really are quite remarkable, Nancy. I'm going to go and call our guests for tomorrow right now. Luncheon should be quite enlightening."

"I hope so," said Nancy. "I certainly hope so."

"Would you pass the rolls, please?" asked Commander Daindridge. He smiled at the others seated around the dining room table.

"June, I'm glad I accepted your invitation," he said. "The rolls are wonderful, the turkey is superb, and the salad is—"

"Ambrosia!" Bess called out.

The commander seemed amused at her enthusiasm. "Yes," he said slowly. "Ambrosia is an excellent word to describe the salad."

"I'm so glad you're enjoying yourself, Adam." Miss Braden was beaming with pride. "With compliments like this, you can eat here anytime you'd like."

She turned to the moody individual on her left. "Are you enjoying your meal, Sam? You've hardly touched your food."

Sam Beaumont looked up from his plate. "Oh, excuse me, June. I—I guess I'm still feeling a little embarrassed."

"About what, Sam?" Miss Braden asked.

"How I acted toward Laura's friends the other day." The lobsterman turned to Nancy, Bess, and George. "I'm really sorry about my behavior. As anybody will probably tell you, I'm not the most sociable person you'll ever meet."

"That's all right, Mr. Beaumont," said Nancy. "We understand." She glanced at her friends, knowing that they were wondering the same thing. Was this all an act, or was Sam Beaumont really a nice guy?

Nancy decided to test him out.

"Maybe you can take us out on your boat sometime," she said. "Just around the area, of course."

"That would be a pleasure," Sam replied.

"Could we go to Craven Cove?" asked Nancy.

She watched Sam Beaumont closely for his reaction, but she saw no change on his face before Commander Daindridge spoke up.

"You girls really should stay away from that spot," he warned. "It's not safe. The currents are very

118

tricky, especially around the lighthouse. They probably contributed to Karl's accident."

"I have a feeling something else caused Mr.
Braden's engine to *blow up.*" Nancy was throwing out
bait, hoping someone would bite.

"You mean the way yours did?" the commander
asked. Nancy noticed that the commander did not
react to the information that Braden's boat was blown
up. Perhaps he already knew, she decided.

"The Coast Guard has confirmed that your boat
was tampered with," he continued.

"They have?" Bess said, amazed.

Nancy thought her friend's eyes were just a bit too
wide to be believed. Bess was obviously putting on an
act, trying to help get information.

"Yes," the commander replied. "I'm sure the sheriff's office will be contacting you as soon as he's
notified."

"How did you hear about this if the sheriff doesn't
even know yet?" Nancy asked.

Commander Daindridge winked. "I'm in the intel-
ligence business, young lady. We hear things before
they're even said."

Everybody at the table laughed except Sam Beaumont. The solemn-faced man only sipped his coffee
and glanced at Laura, who had taken the day off work
to join the lunch party. Nancy could tell that something was on his mind, but she had no idea what.

"I'm going to get the dessert," Laura announced.
"Nancy, would you give me a hand?"

"Sure, Laura," Nancy replied. She rose quickly from her seat and followed the girl into the kitchen.

"Why don't you tell Commander Daindridge and Uncle Sam about the code?" Laura asked Nancy. "Maybe they can help figure it out."

Nancy let out a deep sigh. "I know this is hard for you, Laura, but I can't. Don't you see? One of them might be the person we're after."

"But that's impossible!" Laura exclaimed. "Dad has known Uncle Sam most of his life. And he has been friends with the commander for years."

"That doesn't mean one of them couldn't be guilty," Nancy said.

"No," said Laura. "I can't believe it. I'll bet it's Ms. Walters, or somebody else. But not one of them."

Nancy didn't know what to say. It was obvious that Laura didn't want to think her friends might be out to hurt her.

"Please tell them," Laura begged. "Whatever danger my father is in could get worse very soon. Please show them the code, or I will."

"Code?" came a harsh voice from behind them.

Nancy turned to find Sam Beaumont looming in the doorway. He'd heard everything. And the stormy look in his eyes told Nancy the code was something he wanted to see very badly.

13

Return to Craven Cove

Sam Beaumont strode into the kitchen. "Did you say you found a code? Where is it?"

Nancy had to think quickly. "It's nothing, Mr. Beaumont," she replied. "In fact, Miss Braden said it was probably a code her brother made up as a boy."

Nancy hoped Laura would go along with her story, but she wasn't sure. She could tell the girl was filled with doubt.

"Is that true, Laura?" Sam Beaumont asked. He moved closer to her.

Laura hesitated for a minute. "Yes, it's true," she answered. "Aunt June *did* say that."

Beaumont didn't look convinced. "May I see the code?"

"Nancy has it," Laura replied.

Nancy quickly grabbed some dessert plates and put them in Beaumont's hands. "Here, Mr. Beaumont," she said. "You can carry these, and Laura and I will bring the cake and drinks."

The lobsterman frowned. "But I'd really like to——"

"We can't keep everyone waiting," Nancy said. She was talking very fast, trying to keep from answering any questions. "Especially my friend Bess. Her meal isn't complete without dessert."

Nancy handed the three-layer coconut cake to Laura. Then she picked up a tray of coffee and soft drinks. "Let's go." She moved quickly toward the doorway.

"Nancy." Sam's voice was low and menacing. "You don't know what you're playing with. That code could be dangerous to someone."

The menacing tone in Beaumont's voice and the cold look in his eyes made Nancy nervous. She didn't know what the coded message was, but she knew now that it was important—at least to Sam Beaumont.

"You may be right, Mr. Beaumont," Nancy said, trying to sound very calm and cheerful. "But I won't know that until I decode it."

Nancy turned and stepped into the foyer, then stopped short. Standing just outside the kitchen door was Commander Daindridge. Had he been listening?

The naval officer smiled in a very friendly way. "I was just coming to see if you needed any help."

"That's why *I* came back here, Adam." Sam Beaumont stepped into view, followed by Laura.

122

"That's very good, Sam," said the commander easily. "You carry the plates, and I'll carry these." Politely he took the tray of drinks from Nancy. "If you don't mind, of course, Ms. Drew."

"Not at all, Commander." Nancy felt as if she were caught between two forces. The commander and Sam Beaumont seemed to be studying each other. Maybe they were working together, because both of them looked as if they had something to hide.

"You know, Nancy," the commander said as he and Nancy moved ahead of Sam and Laura, "decoding is my specialty. Maybe I can help you with this message you've found."

Great, Nancy told herself. Now everybody knows about the code. "That won't be necessary," Nancy told him sweetly. "It's really just an old puzzle."

"Is that so?" The commander raised an eyebrow. Nancy got the feeling he did not believe her.

"That looks absolutely yummy," Bess said as soon as she saw the cake. "And I've saved just enough room for a little piece or two."

As the dessert was being served, Nancy was thinking about Braden's code.

Karl Braden had gone to a lot of trouble to hide the code from everyone, she thought. And now her two main suspects knew about it. They even knew that she had the code. If it really *was* important, then someone would be coming after it soon.

Nancy looked around the table. Bess, George, and Miss Braden were having a great time.

Laura was not. Sam seemed to be questioning her without mercy. Nancy knew he must be grilling her about the code.

She was just about to interrupt them when Commander Daindridge leaned toward her.

"I think we should talk, Nancy." The commander seemed deadly serious. "You may have found something that pertained to Karl's work. He was in naval security, and it's your duty to turn that message in."

Nancy felt cornered. What if the code *did* have something to do with naval security? Did she really have the right to keep it from the commander?

She was just about to answer when the telephone rang.

"I'll get it," said Laura, rushing from the table. Nancy knew she was probably thrilled to get away from Sam Beaumont.

"As I was saying, Ms. Drew," the commander continued, "it's your——"

"Commander Daindridge," Laura called from the kitchen. "It's for you."

Everyone watched as he rose from the table to take the call. Immediately, George moved over to sit next to Nancy.

"Is everything all right?" George whispered.

"Not really," Nancy replied. She told her friend what had happened.

"Oh, that's just great." George shook her head. "What do we do now?"

At that moment Commander Daindridge came

124

back into the room. "That was nothing, folks, but I do feel I have to return to the base," he said. "I just remembered a meeting I have at three."

"I'm sorry to hear that," said Miss Braden. "We've enjoyed having you here."

"Maybe we can do this again," Commander Daindridge replied. "Real soon."

He smiled, said his goodbyes, and headed out of the dining room. Just before he stepped outside, he stopped to look back at Nancy. He fixed her with a sharp gaze, then he nodded once and left.

A few seconds later they heard Commander Daindridge's car pull out of the driveway.

Sam Beaumont suddenly rose from the table. "I think I'd better be going, too," he said.

"Everybody's leaving all at once," Miss Braden said. "I hope it wasn't my cake."

"Of course not," Sam replied. "It was just as good as the ones you made when we were kids."

"And you and Karl would try to sneak a piece after school," Miss Braden recalled. "My mother was always chasing you two."

"So was mine," Beaumont replied. He looked sad for a moment.

"Well," he said finally. "Thank you for everything." He turned and looked from Nancy to Laura. "Think about what I said, Laura. I might be able to help."

Then he nodded to everyone and left the house.

"What was all that about?" Bess asked Laura.

Laura slumped down in her chair, looking very depressed. "Uncle Sam wouldn't stop asking me about that code. He kept saying that people might get hurt if I didn't give it to him. He was like a different person. So pushy, and—and—"

"Threatening?" George asked.

"Yes," Laura muttered.

"That proves it!" Bess exclaimed. "Sam Beaumont is the guilty man."

"Guilty of what?" said Miss Braden. She looked at Nancy. "Did you learn anything new from this little gathering?"

"I think so," Nancy replied softly. "All along I've been unsure of what the crime was, and without that knowledge, I couldn't really figure out anything." Nancy reached into her blouse pocket and removed the sheet of paper containing the code.

"I think I finally know what's going on," she told the others excitedly. "This code is our big break."

Miss Braden sat down at the table and leaned toward Nancy. "Please tell us."

Nancy's eyes were bright with excitement. "Karl Braden must have found out that something terrible was going on at Craven Cove—probably involving smuggling. He started investigating and discovered that someone he knew was involved."

"That's why he hid that code!" Bess exclaimed. "It had something to do with the crook. He didn't know who to trust."

Miss Braden lowered her head. "I wish Karl had trusted me. Maybe I could have helped."

"He couldn't tell you anything," Nancy said. "It would have put you and Laura in too much danger."

"So he hid the code." George drummed her fingers on the tabletop. "Then what?"

Nancy studied the code for a moment. The jumbled numbers and letters still looked like a language from outer space. Then she had an idea.

"Laura, what was the exact date of your father's accident?" Nancy asked eagerly.

"The twenty-eighth of March," Laura replied.

Nancy ran her finger along the page, then stopped. "And what time of night?"

Laura shifted in her seat. "Daddy went out around four o'clock. The storm hit around seven."

"That's what I thought!" Nancy smiled triumphantly as she pointed to a section of the code. "Three, twenty-eight—seven, three, zero."

"Wow!" George gasped. "March twenty-eighth, seven-thirty. This is a message to set up a meeting of some kind!"

"A meeting that my brother didn't want to miss— for any reason," Miss Braden added.

"I think your brother expected to learn the identity of the culprit," Nancy explained.

Bess turned to Laura. "And your father's boat went down off the cove. That must have been where the meeting was to take place."

"But remember," Nancy said, "Karl Braden's boat was sabotaged. The engine blew up. That means the crooks must have found out that he was on to them."

"And the man who first mentioned sabotage was Sam Beaumont," George said. She put her hand on Laura's shoulder. "I'm sorry."

"I just can't believe he'd do this—whatever it is," Laura whispered, her face made whiter by the contrast to her dark hair.

"Neither can I," said Miss Braden. She squeezed Laura's hand. "Sam and my brother were too close."

"So what do we do now?" Bess asked.

Nancy jumped up and ran to the hall closet. "There are still some unanswered questions," she said, grabbing her jacket and the flashlight. "And since everything points back to Craven Cove, I think that's where we have to go for our answers."

"But why are you taking the flashlight?" Bess asked, getting up for her own coat.

"Because there isn't any light in that cave," Nancy replied. "And I have an idea that that's where we should start looking."

"Cave?" A frightened look appeared on Bess's face.

"Sure," Nancy replied. "Sabotage, mysterious codes—why not a cave?"

"All this to catch some smugglers," Bess grumbled.

"Smugglers!" Nancy exclaimed. She shook her head. "No way. Commander Daindridge put me on the right track—naval security. I don't think we're after smugglers, Bess. I think we're after spies!"

14

The Secret in the Cave

"Spies?" said George. "Nancy, how did you figure it out?"

"Later, George. Now we just have to get going."

Miss Braden started toward the kitchen. "I'm not going with you," she said. "Someone should be here in case you need to call for help."

"All right, Miss Braden," Nancy said, rushing to the door. "Thanks for lunch. See you later."

George gently pushed Bess ahead of her. "'Bye, Miss Braden."

Just as the girls were climbing into their car, Laura ran out of the house.

"I'm going, too," she said. "I'm sure my father's still out there, and I've got to help him."

"Hop in," said Bess. "The more, the scarier!"

* * *

A thick, damp fog had started rolling in off the water. The sea was choppy. It rose and fell with an eerie, almost hypnotic grace.

"If any of you are frightened," Nancy said at the entrance to the cave, "I can go in alone."

"What if something happened to you?" Bess said. "We'd never forgive ourselves." She clenched her teeth. "Okay, let's go."

Nancy flicked on a flashlight and aimed it into the cave. It appeared to be about six feet high and five feet wide. The beam of light reflected off jagged gray walls, which were damp and covered with green moss in places.

The floor, which slanted down and to the right, was dirt and rock.

"Be careful, everyone," Nancy warned. "And stay together. I heard there are several tunnels in here. We don't want to get separated."

Cautiously, Nancy and the others stepped into the gloomy cave.

No one seemed sure what they were looking for. Nancy told the others to watch for any sign that someone had been using the cave as a hiding place, or as a rendezvous.

It was Nancy who found the first clue. "Look at this!" she called.

"What is it?" Bess asked.

"It's the spot where I stumbled the other day."

"You mean when I saw my father," Laura said.

"Right," Nancy answered. "Remember when I said I'd gotten some dirt on me?" Laura nodded. "Well, it wasn't dirt." Nancy rubbed her hand across a large black stone. A thick black coating smeared on her hand.

"It's some kind of soot," Nancy explained. She moved the stone back farther to reveal a small black pot behind it. There were wires and a timing device attached to the pot.

"What is it?" asked Laura, running her finger over the device.

"An electronic smoke bomb," Nancy said. She let the rock fall back into place. "Someone may use it to signal when the coast is clear."

"Why not use a flashlight?" Laura asked.

"This way the person doesn't have to be here," Nancy explained. "He just sets the clock and leaves."

Nancy stood up and moved farther into the cave. "Now let's find out if there's a special hiding place."

The others followed Nancy into the darkness, stepping very slowly and carefully.

As the girls moved along, they searched the cracks and crevices, hoping to find another clue.

Several times each of them stumbled, but they kept on going.

Finally the girls came to a steep slope leading down into a small chamber.

"Be careful," warned Nancy. "The ground is wet and slippery here."

Nancy went first, followed by Laura, Bess, and George. Soon they were standing in a room that appeared to have been carved out of solid rock.

Nancy flashed the light around the chamber. To their right were two other tunnels. Both of them looked darker than the room they were in. From somewhere deep within those tunnels, the girls could hear the roar of the ocean.

Bess shivered. "This must be where smugglers in the old days hid their stolen goods," she said.

"Colonial soldiers used to hide in here, too," Laura added. She looked around the room, amazed. "My father told me about this place, but he never brought me here."

"I don't like this," Nancy said, frowning.

Bess moved closer to the others. "Neither do I."

"I mean I don't like this." Nancy aimed the flashlight at the floor. There were pools of water all around them, rapidly growing in size.

"This must be one of the rooms that fills up with water," Nancy said.

"Then why would smugglers in the old days use it?" Laura asked.

"Because it only fills up a little bit," Nancy answered. "See?" She pointed the light at the base of the walls. "The wet rocks and algae show how high the water rises." The marks Nancy indicated were about waist high.

"Well, let's hurry and look around so we can get out of here," Bess urged.

Nancy moved forward a few steps. "Whatever we're looking for would have to be hidden above the water line so it wouldn't get damaged."

Slowly Nancy played the light along the walls, until she spotted a small shelf of rock about five feet off the ground.

Nancy walked over to examine the piece of jutting rock. "Nothing here," she said with a sigh. Then she ran her fingers along the large cracks nearby.

"I've got something!" Nancy cried. Quickly she dug her fingers into one of the cracks and pulled. She dislodged a small piece of rock to reveal a hidden space about twenty inches deep. Cautiously Nancy aimed the light inside.

What she saw made her smile. "Look at this," she exclaimed, reaching for a sleek metal and plastic attaché case. Embossed on the front was the U.S. Navy insignia.

George moved in for a better look. "It *is* navy secrets that are being stolen! How did you—"

Nancy examined the case carefully. "There's a combination lock on it," she said.

"Are you going to open it?" Laura asked.

"Not here," Nancy replied. "If spies are truly involved in this, the attaché case could be booby-trapped. I think we'll let the authorities handle it."

Suddenly the girls heard the sound of footsteps moving quite swiftly through the tunnel.

133

"Someone is moving this way," Bess whispered loudly. She was obviously trying her best not to scream.

But Laura couldn't hold back her fear. "Maybe we can get out through one of the other tunnels," she almost shouted.

"No!" Nancy grabbed Laura's arm.

"Don't try it," came a deep, masculine voice. "The tunnels are filling with water. You'd drown before you found your way out."

Everyone recognized the voice immediately. It was Sam Beaumont's.

"I think you'd better wait right where you are." Beaumont's voice echoed off the walls. "Don't move. I'm coming to you."

Soon the figure of Sam Beaumont filled the entrance to the chamber.

He was carrying a kerosene lantern that cast an eerie glow throughout the room. The flickering flame caused shadows to dance across the walls.

The lobsterman glared at the girls. "I warned you that this could get dangerous."

"We had to take that chance, Mr. Beaumont." Nancy tried to sound confident as her eyes darted all over the room. She was trying to find a way to escape. She wasn't sure what Sam Beaumont would do, but she felt she had to be ready.

"So what have you learned, Nancy Drew?" Sam asked.

"I've deduced that somebody is stealing navy

secrets," Nancy replied calmly. "And using this place to pass those secrets on."

Sam Beaumont moved farther into the room.

"I've also just about decided that Laura's father found out about it and tried to track the spies down," Nancy continued. "Unfortunately, they found out and blew his boat up to keep him from talking."

George inched closer to Nancy. "Why are you telling him all of this?" she whispered.

"I've got a hunch," said Nancy. "Trust me."

Sam Beaumont eased down the slope and approached the girls. Bess and George stepped back, but Nancy and Laura stood their ground.

"Karl and I used to play here when we were boys," Sam said. "We pretended to be pirates and smugglers. If we'd only known then . . ." His voice trailed off.

He stood looking around for a minute, then removed a slip of paper from his coat pocket and handed it to Laura.

She took the note in trembling hands and read it silently. When she'd finished, her eyes were wide with disbelief. She seemed unable to say a word as she slipped the paper in her jeans pocket.

Sam Beaumont broke the silence. "Follow me," he ordered. The lobsterman started out of the room and the girls trailed close behind him. When Sam reached the top of the slope, he turned. "Come on—quick now. It's going to get mighty wet in here."

Laura walked beside Nancy for a moment, then suddenly bolted forward to walk with Sam.

Nancy and the others followed him through the tunnel without speaking. She could tell that Bess and George were filled with questions, but they weren't saying a thing. Nancy was glad.

The fog was very thick when they emerged from the cave. Nancy looked down at the shoreline and spotted a small motorboat bouncing on the rough sea. It did appear to be anchored to the beach.

"Is that yours, Mr. Beaumont?" she asked.

"It's half mine," Sam Beaumont replied. "The other half belongs to a friend."

Nancy had an excellent guess who that friend was.

"Where are we going?" Bess asked as they headed down the side of the cliff. "And what was in that note Sam gave Laura?"

Nancy looked out across the cove. "I'd say we're going to have a boat ride and then maybe a big surprise."

The girls and Sam Beaumont scrambled across the wet and sagging dock at the abandoned lighthouse. The crossing had been difficult, and all of them were cold and wet.

Nancy, Bess, and George followed Laura and Sam into the old lighthouse.

Once inside, Laura stopped only long enough to catch her breath. Then she took off for the stairs.

Sam Beaumont had to yell out a warning. "Be careful to walk on the right side. The other part of the stairs has caved in a bit."

Nancy watched as Laura inched past the damaged section of the stairs and raced up the rest.

When they had almost reached the top, Bess asked Nancy, "Why wouldn't Laura show us what was in the note?"

"Because," Nancy replied, "she wanted to make sure it was true first."

In the dim light of the lantern, Bess and George stood next to Nancy in stunned silence. There were *three* people in the center of the lighthouse tower. Sam Beaumont was leaning against the old lamp casing. And a few feet from him was Laura Braden— her arms wrapped around a tall, handsome man who was hugging her tightly.

Nancy smiled. "Bess and George, meet Karl Braden."

15

Terror in the Lighthouse

Karl and Laura Braden held each other for a long time.

Watching them, Nancy's mind was filled with warm thoughts about her own father.

We're going to spend some time together when I get back home, Dad, Nancy promised herself.

When Laura finally pulled back from her father, the girls could see tears running down her cheeks. "Nancy, Bess, George," Laura said between sniffles, "this is my dad."

"Pleased to meet you, Mr. Braden," said Nancy. "We've heard *a lot* about you."

"And I've heard a lot about you, also," Karl Braden replied, nodding toward Sam Beaumont. Braden grinned and shook hands with the girls.

Laura's father was about six feet tall and fairly well built. But the months of hiding and running had clearly left their mark on him. He looked very tired and gaunt.

The naval officer motioned for the girls to sit on the floor. Laura sat beside him and he hugged her close. He whispered something to Sam Beaumont, who nodded and quickly went down the stairs.

"Sorry about the accommodations," Karl Braden said. "This has been home for a while."

"I know," said Nancy.

"I'm not surprised," Braden replied. "You've proven yourself to be very resourceful." Then he frowned. "I'm glad you're all here, but I'm afraid you're in great danger."

Laura threw her arms around his neck. "Daddy, what is this all about?"

Karl Braden sighed. "It's about a friend turned traitor to his country. A little over six months ago I discovered that—"

"Commander Daindridge was selling naval secrets," Nancy interrupted.

"Yes." The look on Karl Braden's face told Nancy how surprised he was that she knew.

"It all came together this evening," Nancy explained. "Once I knew that the naval base was the target, then I figured out who the criminal was."

"It still could have been Mr. Beaumont," said George.

"Not really," Nancy replied. "If Laura's father had

suspected Mr. Beaumont, he would have told his commanding officer. After all, naval security was at stake. But he didn't tell Commander Daindridge. That proved which man he suspected."

"That's true," Braden agreed. "I'd been watching Adam for some time, but I had no real proof. And I didn't know who else might be involved."

"What was he actually stealing?" George asked. She had curled up next to the lantern as if she were about to listen to a campfire story.

"Information that we received through radio communications," Karl Braden replied. "The secret locations of our nuclear submarines." He leaned back against the wall. "Adam decoded the messages, copied them, and left them at some rendezvous place."

"But you didn't know where that was," Nancy said.

"Not at first, but after following Adam for a while, I realized he came to the cove a lot. I started talking to people in the area."

"The Gessups," said Bess.

"That's right." Gently Karl Braden brushed Laura's hair away from her face with his hand. "Then I got hold of a secret message that set up Daindridge's next drop. I hid it in an old code book of mine at home. But he found out what I had done and somehow rigged my boat to—"

"Explode." Once again Nancy surprised the naval officer. She could see that he was becoming more and more impressed.

"He did the same thing to me and my friends," Nancy explained. "When he thought we were getting too close."

Karl Braden lowered his head for a moment, then looked up at Nancy. "Sam told me about that. I'm sorry my problem put you in so much danger."

"Don't worry about it," Nancy said. She smiled slightly. "We did it to help Miss Braden and Laura. You and Laura mean a lot to her." Suddenly Nancy became serious again. "Now please tell us what happened after the explosion."

"The boat went down," Karl Braden continued. "Luckily, I was able to swim to this lighthouse. I hid out here for a week, then left town."

"But why, Daddy? Why didn't you come to Aunt June and me, or the police?"

Karl Braden took Laura's face in his hands. "Because I was dealing with very dangerous men, sweetheart. They wouldn't have stopped at hurting you or June to get to me. And I didn't know who might be working with Daindridge at the base, so I couldn't go there." He sighed heavily. "It was best that everyone thought I was dead."

"Why'd you come back, then?" George asked.

"For two reasons," Braden replied. "Because I missed Laura, and because I couldn't let Daindridge continue to get away with his treachery."

"So you contacted Sam Beaumont," Nancy guessed.

"Yes," Braden replied. "Sam brought me food and clothing. And he was my eyes and ears. He kept tabs on Daindridge and Laura. Everything went well until Laura spotted me a couple of times. I couldn't seem to stay away."

"Then people started thinking about you again," said Nancy. "And after we started nosing around, Daindridge began to suspect that you were alive."

"I knew what he'd do, so Sam and I started sending you warnings."

"The necklace," Laura said, clapping her hand to her mouth.

"And the albatross," Braden added. He turned to Nancy. "It was a bit melodramatic, but I was hoping it would scare you enough to stop your investigation. I needed time to get more evidence against Daindridge."

"His secret meeting place is in the cave on the ledge," said Laura.

"I know that, sweetheart," Braden replied. "But I couldn't locate the exact spot where he hid the stolen documents."

"Nancy did," Bess piped up.

Nancy quickly told Laura's father about the secret compartment in the cave wall and the attaché case they had discovered.

"Where is it now?" Karl Braden asked.

"We left it in its hiding place, because I thought it might be booby-trapped," Nancy replied. "We were going to go for the police, but Mr. Beaumont arrived just then."

"So all we have to do is get the case and—" George began.

Suddenly everyone heard a shout and a loud, crashing sound.

Nancy sprang to her feet. "Someone's hurt! Who's downstairs?"

"Sam is," Braden replied. Immediately he rose to his feet, grabbed the lantern, and started down the stairs. "I asked him to guard the place!"

Quickly but cautiously, the girls hurried down the steps behind Laura's father.

Nancy felt a terrible sense of dread as she and the others rounded the last curve. She had a feeling she already knew what they would find at the bottom of the stairs.

Sure enough, there on the floor was the body of Sam Beaumont. He was lying facedown and very still.

Karl Braden reached him first and examined his friend carefully. "He's been hit over the head, but he's alive," he said, sounding relieved.

"But what was that loud banging we heard?" Bess asked.

Everyone looked around. Then Nancy yelled, "The door!" She and Karl Braden pushed on the outside door, but it wouldn't budge.

"Hello in there," came a voice from outside. It was Commander Daindridge. "Can you hear me?"

"I hear you, Adam," Karl yelled back. He beat on the door with his fists. "This is between you and me. Let these kids go."

"No way, Karl," said the commander. "Too many witnesses."

"We'll get out, and we'll tell everything!" Laura shouted.

"Not likely," came the cool reply. "By the way, thanks, girls, for leading me to Karl. I'm surprised that you, Nancy, believed my little meeting story."

"You followed us!"

"That's right, and in about five minutes, you and your newfound knowledge will be nothing but a memory."

"What do you mean, Adam?" Karl asked. His voice was filled with anger.

"I've planted a few bombs around the base of the lighthouse while you were having your happy little reunion. I've locked all the doors, including the one to the lighthouse keeper's cottage."

Everyone inside the lighthouse froze. No one knew what was safe to touch anymore.

"Sorry it has to end this way, *old friend*. But that's spy business."

"Was Ms. Walters involved with you and your spying?" Nancy asked.

"No. I was just giving her false information so she'd go around in circles. You, Ms. Drew, aren't so easy to fool. Au revoir."

A moment later the girls and Karl Braden heard the sound of a powerful motorboat fire up.

"Nancy, do you think he really meant it?" Laura's eyes were filled with fear.

Before Nancy could answer, they all heard another sound—the faint ticking of the bombs' timing devices. The steady chorus of clicks was steadily marking off the minutes to their destruction.

16

Homecoming

Nancy's eyes darted around the room. To her right, Bess and George had managed to revive Sam Beaumont. He was getting up and shaking off the blow.

Karl and Laura Braden were pushing against the heavy wooden outer door, trying to break through. It was no use.

"They made these doors to withstand the sea," Karl said. "Adam put a padlock on this door as well. We're not going to break through there."

"How about the door to the cottage?" asked Nancy.

Braden ran over and slammed against it a few times. "It's made the same way," he said. "There was a key in this lock. Adam must have used it, then thrown it away."

"Wait a minute!" Nancy exclaimed. "Did you say that Commander Daindridge locked the door?"

"Yes," Braden replied, "but he took the key."

Quickly Nancy reached into her jacket pocket and pulled out a small black case. She opened it and moved toward the door and began removing a series of thin metal probes.

"A lock-picking kit!" Karl Braden said in amazement.

"And Nancy knows how to use it," Bess said with pride. She crossed her fingers. "If we've got enough time, Nancy can get us out of here."

Nancy wished she was as confident as her friend. Perspiration trickled down her forehead, but her hands were steady.

She wasn't sure if she could pick the lock, even if there *was* enough time. But she was determined to try. Slowly she slipped one of the thin wires into the lock and moved it around. She could feel it catch on the lock mechanism, but she couldn't seem to get the lock to release.

"Maybe we'd better go back up to the tower," Laura suggested. "At least we'll be farther away from the blast."

"But the tower will fall in when the bombs go off," Nancy replied, still fiddling with the lock. "The only place we'll be safe is out of here."

"Nancy!" Laura exclaimed. She paused for a moment, as if she were listening to something. Then she said, "I think the ticking is getting faster!"

147

Sam Beaumont moaned from the corner. "We've got only a few minutes left. I'm sorry he got past me, Karl," Nancy heard him say. "I didn't hear him until it was too late."

Again Nancy carefully twisted the probe inside the lock. She realized she was holding her breath as she moved it slightly and pushed. *Click.* The tumbler slipped into place, and a second later, the door flew open.

"Hurry!" Nancy shouted, switching on her flashlight and entering the cottage. She swept the light across the floor, looking for traps, but she didn't see any.

George, Bess, and Laura hurried into the cottage behind her, followed by Karl, who was helping Sam Beaumont.

Instantly Nancy found the front door and flung it open.

With Nancy leading the way, everyone raced around the base of the lighthouse. They knew they had only seconds to reach the safety of the open sea.

As they rounded the lighthouse and headed for the dock, Nancy looked back. She spotted four large black boxes attached to the side of the lighthouse. Now she knew that Adam Daindridge had been deadly serious.

As quickly as they could, everyone crammed into Sam's motorboat. Karl pulled it away from the dock. The waves were choppy and the tide was going against them.

"Come on," Nancy urged the boat under her breath. "Please move faster."

Then they heard it: a deafening explosion followed by a brilliant flash of light that lit up the dark sky.

Nancy saw flames from the lower half of the lighthouse shoot out across the grounds. They completely destroyed the cottage and almost reached the dock.

Seconds later the tall, ancient structure crumbled at its base and slowly collapsed into itself. The lighthouse crashed to the ground and disintegrated into individual bricks.

"Thank you, Nancy Drew," Karl Braden said softly.

"Don't thank me yet," said Nancy. "We've still got one more thing to do. Look!"

Nancy pointed toward Craven Cove. A small, high-powered speedboat was heading for shore.

"That's Adam!" Karl Braden shouted over the roar of the waves. The boat bobbed violently up and down in the water.

"He's probably heading for the cave," Nancy said. "We've got to catch him before he escapes with the attaché case."

She reached for the two-way radio. "I'm going to call for the Coast Guard."

While Nancy tried to find assistance, Karl Braden steered the boat toward shore.

With the throttle open full, Sam's vessel skipped across the water at tremendous speed. Karl Braden really knew how to handle the boat, even in extremely rough waters. They reached the cove only seconds after Commander Daindridge.

The spy had jumped out of his boat and begun running along the beach.

Nancy wasn't far behind. As Karl Braden was pulling the boat up on the sand, she leapt from it. Nancy raced after Daindridge with Karl Braden right behind her.

Daindridge saw them coming and quickly abandoned his attempt to reach the cliff. Instead, he bolted for the woods, just beyond the beach. But before he could reach the safety of the trees, Nancy tackled him from behind.

Karl Braden reached down and caught him in an arm lock. Nancy slipped the drawstring out of the hem of her windbreaker.

Sam Beaumont helped Nancy and Karl secure Commander Daindridge with the string.

"It's over, Commander," Nancy told him. "We know what you've been doing. The Coast Guard is on its way."

Just then a Coast Guard cutter appeared in the cove. Its powerful searchlight illuminated the unusual scene on the beach. A siren sounded on the beach road. A few minutes later Miss Braden stepped onto the beach with the police officer.

Nancy watched as Laura went running to meet her aunt. Then she turned back to her prisoner.

"You can't prove a thing," Daindridge snarled.

"I have proof that I've been putting together, Adam," Laura's father snapped back.

"And there's the attaché case in the cave," Nancy added calmly. "I'm sure it has your fingerprints all over it. And if that's not enough, there are six people here who will press charges against you for attempted murder."

"And don't forget willful destruction of public property," Bess put in. "I bet someone is going to be real upset about that lighthouse."

The sheriff picked him up and led him off to the squad car.

"That was the closest and most frightening call I've ever had," said Bess. She looked across the water at the blazing remains of the lighthouse.

"Me, too," said George.

Nancy threw her arms around her two friends and nodded toward the three Bradens' reunion. "Maybe it was," she told them, "but it was definitely worth it."

The next morning the Braden household was still celebrating.

Laura and Miss Braden had gotten up early and fixed a fantastic breakfast feast for Karl, Nancy, Bess, and George. Sam Beaumont had come over, too, talking easily with Karl and Laura. Once or twice he even gave a short, gruff laugh.

The dining table was filled with heaping plates of fruit salad and fresh-baked muffins. The scent of Canadian bacon filled the air, along with scrambled eggs and coffee.

As everyone gathered around the table, Miss Braden raised her glass to give a toast.

"To Nancy, Bess, and George," she said. She gazed at the girls with obvious pride and affection. "Thank you for coming to our rescue, across so many miles and after so many years."

Nancy felt very embarrassed as she smiled and sipped her juice. Then she suddenly remembered a question she had for her old teacher.

"Miss Braden, the sheriff said that you called him before the Coast Guard," Nancy said. "How did you know we were in trouble down at the cove?"

The teacher smiled as she calmly buttered a roll. "Well, I just couldn't believe that Sam was guilty of anything. I've known him too long." She winked at her old friend, who grinned. "I figured if he *was* involved somehow, he was probably helping Karl. I called his local grocery store and asked about his recent shopping habits. Sure enough, the woman there told me that Sam had been buying double his normal amount of food."

Bess was amazed. "Then you knew that he'd been helping to hide your brother," she said slowly.

"Exactly," Miss Braden replied. "And as soon as I knew for sure that Sam was innocent, I figured that Adam was guilty."

"But how did you know we were in trouble?" Nancy persisted.

Miss Braden puckered up her face. "That nosy reporter called. She asked if Commander Daindridge was still here. He hadn't shown up at the base for a meeting with her.

"Anyway, then I drove by Adam's house. His car was there, but his boat was gone. That's when I called the police."

"You have to notice everything," Nancy said softly. She smiled at her former teacher.

"Well," said George, "the naval authorities and the police finally got the commander to talk. He admitted following us to the lighthouse the other day, too. He waited until we went inside and then he set the charge in our boat."

Karl Braden, who had been listening quietly, spoke up. "I want you all to know that I'm sorry about Adam," he said. "But he's going to get what he deserves. And as for me—" He reached for Laura's hand and gave it a squeeze. "I'm going to take some time off and spend it with my family. I've missed them very much."

Laura kissed her father and raised her juice glass. "I'd like to offer another toast. To Nancy Drew, who grew up to become everything my aunt said she would."

"I'm a terrific judge of character," Miss Braden teased.

Laura grinned at her aunt and turned back to

153

Nancy. "Thank you, Nancy," she continued, "for bringing our family back together again."

They all raised their glasses and cheered. Nancy smiled and returned the toast, happy that she had been able to give something back to someone very special to her.